This Is Insane…I Can't Marry Wild Jed Ryder,

Adora Beaudine thought. Until forty-eight hours ago, I hardly knew the man. And he's nothing like my dreams of who I'd marry….

But if she didn't marry him, he'd lose custody of his little sister. And Adora really did believe that would be wrong. So very wrong.

Jed seemed to read her indecision in her eyes. "Never mind. It's a bad idea. Forget it."

"No." She went to him, in the shadows, lifting a hand and clasping his shoulder. She felt like a child on a dare, holding her palm over a flame. She would be burned—and yet nothing seemed so urgent as that she not let go….

Dear Reader,

LET'S CELEBRATE FIFTEEN YEARS
OF SILHOUETTE DESIRE...

with some of your favorite authors and new stars of tomorrow.
For the next three months, we present a spectacular lineup
of unforgettably romantic love stories—led by three
MAN OF THE MONTH titles.

In October, Diana Palmer returns to Desire with
The Patient Nurse, which features an unforgettable hero.
Next month, Ann Major continues her bestselling CHILDREN
OF DESTINY series with *Nobody's Child.* And in December,
Dixie Browning brings us her special brand of romantic
charm in *Look What the Stork Brought.*

But Desire is not only MAN OF THE MONTH! It's new
love stories from talented authors Christine Rimmer,
Helen R. Myers, Raye Morgan, Metsy Hingle and new star
Katherine Garbera in October.

In November, don't miss sensuous surprises from BJ James,
Lass Small, Susan Crosby, Eileen Wilks and Shawna Delacorte.

And December will be filled with Christmas cheer from
Maureen Child, Kathryn Jensen, Christine Pacheco,
Anne Eames and Barbara McMahon.

Remember, here at Desire we've been committed to bringing
you the very best in unforgettable romance and sizzling
sensuality. And to add to the excitement of fifteen wonderful
years, we offer the chance for you to win some wonderful
prizes. Look in the pages at the end of the book for details.

And may we have many more years of happy reading together!

Melissa Senate

Senior Editor

Please address questions and book requests to:
Silhouette Reader Service
U.S.: 3010 Walden Ave., P.O. Box 1325, Buffalo, NY 14269
Canadian: P.O. Box 609, Fort Erie, Ont. L2A 5X3

CHRISTINE RIMMER
THE MIDNIGHT RIDER
TAKES A BRIDE

SILHOUETTE *Desire*®

Published by Silhouette Books

America's Publisher of Contemporary Romance

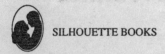

SILHOUETTE BOOKS

ISBN 0-373-76101-5

THE MIDNIGHT RIDER TAKES A BRIDE

Copyright © 1997 by Christine Rimmer

Printed in U.S.A.

CHRISTINE RIMMER

is a third-generation Californian who came to her profession the long way around. Before settling down to write about the magic of romance, she'd been an actress, a salesclerk, a janitor, a model, a phone sales representative, a teacher, a waitress, a playwright and an office manager. Now that she's finally found work that suits her perfectly, she insists she never had a problem keeping a job—she was merely gaining "life experience" for her future as a novelist. Those who know her best withhold comment when she makes such claims; they are grateful that she's at last found steady work. Christine is grateful, too—not only for the joy she finds in writing, but for what waits when the day's work is through: a man she loves who loves her right back and the privilege of watching their children grow and change day to day.

THANKS...
To everyone at the Child Protective Services offices in
both Sierra and Plumas Counties, as well as to
Dan Geffner, Deputy Public Defender in Nevada County.
You all have answered my endless questions so patiently
and I sincerely appreciate your helpfulness.

One

"Honey, all I'm saying is I hope you're not just sitting alone feeling sorry for yourself."

Adora Beaudine tucked the phone beneath her chin and then carefully, *quietly,* blotted her streaming eyes and swiped at her running nose. Yes, she *was* feeling sorry for herself. But that didn't mean her mother had to know.

"Honey, are you there?"

Adora brought the receiver near her mouth again. "Yes, Mom. I'm here."

"Are you all right? You sound so strange, dear."

Adora felt a sob bubbling up. Quickly, she turned to the base of the phone that hung on the wall right behind her and punched the mute button. Then she blew her nose. Then, ignoring the champagne flute in front of her, she reached for the bottle that waited at her elbow and took a long swig.

It tasted lovely, all popping and sparkly, going down. And it should. It was good champagne: Möet & Chandon. Adora had bought it last fall, along with a pair of crystal champagne flutes, right after she'd met Farley Underwood—the rotten, dirty creep. She'd bought it because she'd been utterly certain that one day soon Farley would pop the question. She had pictured them celebrating their engagement with champagne.

But Farley had never popped the question. And now the rat was long gone. And as a birthday present to herself, Adora intended to drink up the evidence of her own folly. Moreover, once she'd emptied the bottle, she meant to smash it—along with both of the crystal flutes.

"Adora? *Adora*..." The voice on the other end of the line had acquired a frantic edge.

Adora turned and gave the mute button a second poke. "I think the connection was bad there for a minute, don't you, Mom?"

"Oh, was that it?"

"Seemed like it to me."

"Well, all I'm telling you is I just don't want you to get bitter. Thirty-five isn't *that* old. I just know this will be the year that you find the right man for you."

Adora had to gulp down another self-pitying sob. Every August eighth for about a decade now, her mother had been telling her that this year she would find "the right man for her."

Her mother went on. "And you know that your family loves you and that we'd all be there for your special day if we could. But your sisters do have their own families to think of now. And Bob and I, well, we've been so terribly busy lately." Bob Shanahan was Lottie Beaudine Shanahan's second husband. Bob had met the widow Beaudine at a Bingo game three and a half years ago. They'd married a few months after that. "We're redoing the house, did I tell you?"

At her mother's mention of redecorating, Adora cast a melancholy glance around the small, bright kitchen where she sat. Farley had taken a hike seven months ago. Since then, to keep depression at bay, Adora had done some redecorating of her own. The old-fashioned cabinets were now a soft white and there were cheery fruits and vegetables stenciled along the ceiling line. It was charming. But it didn't help much. Charming kitchens were supposed to have kids in them. And husbands asking "What's for dinner, hon?"

"Adora. Are you *there?*"

"Yes, Mom. Of course I'm here. And you did tell me you'd been redoing the house."

"The living area is finished. I wish you could see it. All blues and mauves. So soft and inviting. Stylish, yet livable. Bob just loves it...."

Lottie prattled on, about Bob and their four-bedroom, passive-solar house in Tucson and the wonderful, creative things they'd done with the interior. Shamelessly Adora tuned her out. She poured herself a little more champagne, drank it between the "Ums?" and "Umm-hmms" that her mother's monologue required of her, and carefully continued blotting away the stubborn tears that kept leaking from the corners of her eyes.

"And I wish you could see the master bath. Shell pink and pale green. Gold tone fixtures. It's a treat to take a shower...."

From outside on Bridge Street, Adora heard the hard, heavy drone of a big engine—a motorcycle or a souped-up sports car, probably. She listened as it turned into the driveway beside her building, rolled under her kitchen window and stopped in the parking lot out back.

Adora shrugged. Her hairdressing salon downstairs, the Shear Elegance, was closed for the rest of the day. If someone wanted to use one of her parking spaces for a few hours, she supposed it wouldn't hurt anything.

"And I sent you a little something special. Did you get it yet?"

That required actual words for an answer. Adora mustered them. "No, Mom. Not yet."

"Do you have a summer cold or something, Adora? Your nose sounds stuffed up."

Adora went ahead and honked good and loud into her soggy tissue. "Yes, Mom. Now you mention it, I *have* been fighting a cold."

"Oh, honey. Take care of yourself."

"I will."

Right then, someone knocked at the door on the other side of the room. The door led out to a tiny landing and down a narrow set of stairs to the parking lot and also to the back entrance of the Shear Elegance.

"Get some of that nighttime cold medicine," Lottie was suggesting. "The lemony kind you add to hot water. I think it works just great. Bob had a cold last week and I—"

"Listen, Mom. There's someone at the door. I have to go."

"But, Adora—"

"Really. Gotta go."

"Now you call me, when you get that package...."

"I will. Love you." Adora twisted in her chair to hook the phone back in its cradle. Then she faced front with a sigh and picked up her glass of champagne.

There was a second knock at the door.

Adora sipped slowly, looking at the door, thinking that maybe she wouldn't bother to answer it, after all.

She knew who it would be: Lizzie Spooner, her best pal. Lizzie had said she'd be over as soon as she finished her shift at the Superserve Mart. Adora thought the world of Lizzie, but right now she didn't feel like dealing with anyone. She set down her glass. And then, to take her mind off answering the door, she picked up the champagne bottle and began reading the back label.

But then the knock came for a third time, louder and more insistent than before. With another mournful little sigh, Adora rose and went to the door.

She started talking before she even had it all the way open. "Listen, Lizzie, I don't really feel like—" The sentence died in her throat, because it wasn't Lizzie after all.

It was Jed Ryder, whose mother, Lola Pierce, was Adora's single employee at the Shear Elegance downstairs. Adora remembered the loud, pounding sound of that engine she'd heard moments ago and realized it must have been Jed's Harley.

"Oh. Hi." Adora swiped a tear from her cheek and tried a friendly smile.

Jed didn't smile back. And she couldn't see his eyes, because he was wearing a pair of wraparound, black-lensed sunglasses. As always, he looked like the basic definition of the word *dangerous,* dressed in denim and leather, with all that black hair streaming around his massive shoulders and that single diamond stud he always wore glittering in his right ear.

He spoke at last, in that low, eerily gentle voice of his. "Sorry to bother you. But I called the shop downstairs and got no answer."

"I closed up early."

Though she couldn't be sure with those dark shades hiding his eyes, he seemed to be looking at her strangely. Maybe he was wondering about the tear streaks on her cheeks, her runny nose—and the champagne bottle she still clutched in her hand.

He asked in that careful, quiet way of his, "Listen, are you all right?"

"Sure. I'm great. Just terrific." She stuck the bottle under her arm and dug a rumpled tissue from the front pocket of her shorts. Then she wiped her eyes and blew her nose, bending to the side a little, to keep from dropping the champagne.

When she stopped blowing and looked at him again, Jed Ryder had shoved his hands into the pockets of his tight, worn-out jeans. He'd turned his head away, toward the parking lot. And he was actually shuffling his feet in their heavy, black biker boots.

Why, I've made him nervous, she thought.

Adora swiped once more at her nose with a dry corner of the tissue—and hid a smile. To the bikers who sometimes hung out over at the local tavern, Jed was nothing short of a legend. They called him the Midnight Rider. He was a loner and a maverick, even among their kind. A man to be shown respect, a force to be reckoned with.

But he obviously didn't have a clue about how to handle a crying woman.

Adora found the thought that *she* made *him* uncomfortable reassuring. It occurred to her that there was no reason in the world why they had to stand here with the door open to talk. She should let him in.

In response to that idea, she heard her mother's voice, clear as a bell, chiming inside her head: *Adora Sharleen, don't you dare let that Hell's Angel inside your home.*

Adora tucked the tissue away and got a firm grip on

the neck of the champagne bottle. Then she stepped back. "Come on in, why don't you?"

At first he didn't move, except to cant his head sideways as if smelling a trap. She felt certain he would refuse her invitation. But then he shrugged and crossed the threshold. Once inside, he stood looking around cautiously, like a wild animal that had been brought indoors—a careful wild animal, one who suspected he'd made an error to let himself be confined in so small a space.

Adora shut the door, then gestured at her Country French oak table and the four matching chairs around it. "Have a seat."

He shook his head. "I'm just looking for Ma, that's all. I thought maybe you'd know where she is."

"No, I haven't seen her since around one." Adora slid around him and went to a cupboard near the sink. "We had nothing booked for the rest of the day, so I just sent her on home." She spoke over her shoulder as she brought down that other champagne flute, which she filled from the bottle in her hand. Then, feeling naughty, daring and defiant, she turned and held the flute out to him. "Champagne?"

He stood very still. Since the shades masked his eyes and the rest of his face bore no discernable expression, she hadn't a clue as to what he might be thinking. He just looked at her. Or at least, she assumed he was looking at her. For a very long time.

In the end she couldn't stand the silence. Her lip started quivering. She bit it to make it be still and thrust the glass in his direction once more. "Please. Take it."

"Why?"

"We'll have a toast."

One black eyebrow arched up a fraction from behind the mask of the sunglasses. "To what?"

"To...the single life."

He grunted. "What's so great about bein' single?"

The feeling of naughty defiance had evaporated as swiftly as it had come. Now she felt lousy again, about her life and herself—about everything. She also felt just reckless enough to tell him the truth.

"There is nothing great about being single. But maybe if I make a toast to it, I can convince myself not to hate it so much."

His full-lipped mouth, which was surrounded by a well-trimmed and rather soft-looking beard, quirked up just a little at both corners. He peeled off his shades and hooked them on one of the pockets of the black leather vest he wore.

For what seemed like the first time, she met his eyes. They were a beautiful silvery-gray, and startling in contrast to his raven black hair.

He was definitely smiling now. "Bad day, huh?"

The laugh that escaped her came perilously close to being a sob. "*Bad* isn't a strong enough word."

His smile faded. He just waited—for her to go on, she supposed.

So she did. "It's my birthday."

"How old?"

This time her laugh was more of a snort. "Is that any kind of question to ask a woman?"

He started to smile again. "Probably not. As I remember it, you were a few years ahead of me in school."

"Oh, right. Rub it in."

"How old?"

She gave in and confessed, "Thirty-five."

He continued to study her.

She glanced down at the flute she still held. "Look. If you're not going to drink this—"

"Hell." In two steps he stood just inches away. He lifted the glass from her hand.

She blinked and stared up at him. He really was an imposing man, especially this close up. His shoulders went on for days. And from the torn-off sleeves of his denim shirt, his massive arms emerged thick and hard as slabs of granite. Over the shirt, he wore that black leather vest with a thousand zippers and pockets on it. His belt and his boots were of black leather, too. And he also wore fingerless black leather riding gloves. Adora thought she could smell all that leather—which was odd. A moment ago she couldn't have smelled anything; her nose had been plugged solid due to her birthday crying jag.

But Jed Ryder seemed to be the kind of guy who could clear out a woman's sinuses just by stepping up good and close.

A silver cross gleamed on the wedge of sculpted chest between the top two buttons of his shirt. Adora stared at that cross, thinking that she should probably be frightened, here alone with him in her apartment. But he didn't scare her. Maybe because she knew his mother so well, and knew how Lola loved him and counted on him. Or maybe because of Tiffany, his much-younger half-sister. Tiff adored Jed.

Really, who could say why he didn't scare her? He just didn't. Not at all.

He watched her look at him. Then he held out the champagne he'd just taken from her. "Where's yours?" She gestured toward the table behind him. He turned around and scooped up her flute. After handing it to her, he raised his high. "Here's to you. Happy damn birthday, Adora Beaudine."

"Thank you, Jed Ryder." They drank at the same time, not stopping until both of their glasses were empty.

He held out his glass to her, and Adora obligingly refilled it all the way to the rim. Then she poured more for herself as well.

He proposed a second toast. "And here's to you findin' whatever you're looking for." He waited for her to drink with him.

She decided to provide a few specifics first. "A good-looking, upscale kind of guy with a friendly attitude, a steady job and marriage on his mind would be nice."

He actually chuckled at that. They drank again, to the bottom of their glasses, as they had before. She raised the bottle, offering another refill.

But when she tipped it over his glass, only a few drops came out. She made a small sound of regret, then suggested, "I think I have some brandy under the sink."

He shook his head and backed up enough to set his glass on the table. "I gotta go."

She made a tsking sound and shook her head. "Why did I know you'd say that?"

He looked at her in that studied, patient way of his.

She mentally counted to five, giving him a chance to say something. He didn't, so she answered her own question. "I knew you would say that because it's what men are always saying to me. 'I gotta go.' Or, 'I really do have to go.' Or, 'Adora. Back off. I said I'm going now.'"

He was squinting at her a little, as if trying to figure her out. "Aw, come on. It can't be that bad."

"Sure, it can." She turned and plunked the champagne bottle on the counter, then whirled back to face him. "I drive men away. I try too hard. Everybody in town knows it. No one's ever going to marry me. I'm going to be single for the rest of my life." She hadn't set her glass down, so she gestured wildly with it. "All my sisters are married. My mother's *re*married. They've all moved away to other parts of California—or to Arizona, in my mother's case. They've left me alone here in Red Dog City, with my beauty shop and my cute two-bedroom apartment and my simple little dreams of love and a family that are never going to come true. It's pitiful. *I'm* pitiful." She held out both arms then, and looked down at her body. "Just look at me."

He said nothing, as usual. After a moment spent staring at her own pink blouse and flowered shorts, she raised her head and met those startling eyes that gleamed the same burnished silver as the cross around his neck. Something warm and sweet seemed to move inside her for a moment. But then, as swiftly as it had come, the sensation faded.

Adora gulped and told herself that it was nothing. Except possibly the effect of too much champagne.

The silence had gone on for way too long. She broke it. "Well, you had a nice, long look. Now tell me. What's wrong with me?"

"There's nothin' wrong with you. You look fine."

She glared at him, a glare that gradually turned to a glum frown as she realized that she was making a complete fool of herself. Again. She let her head fall back and stared at the ceiling with its darling little rim of marching fruits and vegetables. "Oh, what am I doing?"

"What do you mean?"

"You know." She made herself lower her chin and look at him. "Dragging you in here. Making you drink champagne with me. Telling you things you don't even want to know. I really do have 'desperate woman' written all over me."

He looked uncomfortable. In a moment he'd be shuffling those big, black boots. "Hey. It's all right."

"No, it's not." She leaned back against the counter and ran her finger around the rim of her glass. Then she looked up at him. "But you're a gentleman to say so."

He relaxed and chuckled for the second time, a low, purring growl of a sound.

She smiled in response. "Did I say something funny?"

"Not really. I just don't get called a gentleman too often, that's all."

"Well, you should. 'Cause you are." She pushed away from the counter and stood up straight. "You said you can't find Lola?"

"Yeah."

"Tiff's been with you?"

He nodded. "We went camping over the weekend."

"That's right, Lola said you two had taken off together. And we missed Tiff at the shop today."

Tiff, who was eleven, liked to make herself at home in the shop downstairs, visiting with the customers, helping out with anything the adults would let her do. And some afternoons, when the workday was through, Tiff would come on upstairs. Adora always enjoyed those times. She had grown up with a houseful of sisters, after all. She liked having other females around. Tiff would help Adora with her various decorating projects. They'd drink lemonade. Sometimes Adora would do Tiff's hair. And other days they'd just lie around watching "Oprah" in companionable silence.

Adora asked, "So is Tiff around the corner now?"

"Yeah." Lola and Tiff lived in the small house Jed had bought for them, around the corner from Adora's, on Church Street. "I left her snoozin' on the couch. Poor kid's beat. We hiked all the way to Crystal Falls yesterday and didn't get back to my place until late. Then I had work to do this morning, so Tiff hung around the cabin until I could run her into town." Jed owned a machine shop out on Jackson Pike Road and lived in a cabin right next to it. "Now I gotta get back to check on things at the shop. But I don't want to leave Tiff alone without knowing where Ma's off to."

"You know, before she left today, Lola mentioned that the blackberries are ripe down by Trout Creek. She said that Tiff just loves blackberry pie."

He lifted his shades from where they hung on his vest. "Thanks. I'll check down by the creek next."

Adora watched him as he hid those beautiful eyes once more, remembering all the old rumors about him. He *had* been a wild boy, in trouble all the time.

And, of course, there had been the rape scandal all those years ago, when he'd been caught by Charity Laidlaw in her daughter's bed. That had been an ugly mess, complicated even more by the fact that it had been a family matter; Charity Laidlaw's brother had been Lola's second husband—and Jed's stepfather.

Dangerous, most folks in town called Jed. *Dangerous and bad.*

But no matter what they all said, Jed Ryder was kind at heart to listen so patiently to her self-pitying babble the way he had. And he was so conscientious about his family....

Adora heard herself asking, "You know where the best berries are along Trout Creek?" He shook his head. She set down her empty champagne glass. "Come on, then. I'll show you."

That huge, gleaming chopper of his was waiting, right where she thought it would be, down in the small parking lot behind her shop.

Jed reached for his helmet when they stood beside the thing. "Get on."

Adora took in a long breath. Yes, she knew for sure now that dangerous Jed Ryder was really a very nice man. But that didn't mean she'd let herself be seen on the back of his Harley. In a small town, word got around. And she could do without rumors about the two of them.

"No. I, um, don't have a helmet." She could feel his eyes on her behind the shades and sensed that he knew the real reason she wouldn't ride with him. But he didn't say a word.

"We can walk," she added hastily, not quite daring to look straight at him. "The creek isn't far. And you couldn't take the bike on the trail, anyway. Come on." She started off, and felt a vague sense relief when he fell in step beside her.

They strolled between her building and the next one over, which housed Denita's Donuts. When they reached the sidewalk, they headed north on Bridge Street, past Church Street and on up to River Street, where they turned right. Once around the corner, they left the shops and stores behind. Wood frame houses, most of them two stories high, lined either side of the street.

In the middle of the block they came to the one-lane

bridge that crossed Trout Creek. Adora led the way down the bank to creekside.

The day was cool for August, and in the shade of all the close-growing trees, with the creek bubbling along nearby, it should have been cooler still. But to Adora, the water and all the greenery seemed to make the air uncomfortably moist. Her hair clung to her temples and felt clammy on the back of her neck. They hadn't gone far along the trail when she stopped and began searching her pockets.

"Gotta do something about my hair," she muttered apologetically. "Ah-ha." She came up with a pink ribbon. Swiftly, she tied up her shoulder-length brown curls into a high ponytail. "There. That's better."

Jed Ryder said nothing, only waited patiently until she was ready to move on.

A few minutes later the trail cut up the hillside for quite a long stretch. Though it was rugged going, Adora remembered her manners and never let the branches of dogwood or mountain laurel snap back at the man behind her. Periodically they would stop and call Lola's name. They got no answer.

At last the trail peaked and headed down once more. At the top, panting from the climb, Adora turned back to Jed with a smile. "It's not far now."

Unfortunately she started walking before she bothered to look ahead. On the first step she tripped on an exposed tree root. With a little squeal of alarm, she went flying. Seconds later she landed on her backside in the dirt.

Jed was there immediately, kneeling, taking off his shades and hooking them on his vest. "You okay?"

She groaned. "I'm going to be black-and-blue where the sun don't shine. But I'll survive." She rolled to one side and rubbed the sore place gently. "Ouch. One of these days I'll learn to pay more attention to where I..."

He was watching her, silent as ever, sort of half smiling. She breathed the end of her sentence, barely giving it sound. "...put my feet."

And then words deserted her. And she could have cared less. There was too much going on for her to think about talking.

All at once the air had grown hotter, sweeter, closer. And Jed seemed to...fill up the world. She could smell leather and dust. And she couldn't help noticing the sheen of sweat on his skin. She wanted to reach out her hand and feel his beard, to find out if it was as soft as it looked. To put out her tongue and taste his sweat...

Adora hitched in a tiny gasp. She couldn't believe her own thoughts. Such thoughts weren't like her at all. She'd never had any interest in that sort of thing. Oh, sure, she'd had a lot of boyfriends in all her years of trying to snare herself a husband. But she'd never gone to bed with any of them. Until Farley Underwood—the weasel. And Farley had made a special point of telling her before he left her what a big, fat zero she had been in that department.

And she supposed if she wanted to go ahead and be depressingly honest, that Farley had been right. She'd *wanted* to be good at sex. Because it seemed to be something that a well-rounded woman ought to be good at. And she'd tried her best to convince both Farley and herself that she'd enjoyed making love.

But she hadn't. Not at all. There had just been too much sweating involved—not to mention those unpleasant noises that Farley would make. Yuck. Sometimes the only way to get through it had been to imagine the clever things she could do with window treatments once they were married and had their first house. Or to try to decide whether or not it would be pretentious to monogram their towels.

But right then she could have cared less about window treatments. And monograms were the last thing on her mind. Right then her own sweat felt erotic. And Jed Ryder's sweat looked delicious. And even the air seemed, somehow, to be humming in a way that set every nerve she had singing. Her body felt heavy. And yet quick and ready at the same time.

It was not yucky. Not yucky at all.

It must be the champagne.

But she knew that it wasn't. The trek along the trail had banished the glow she'd felt back at her apartment. She was now plain sober. As well as sexually aroused.

Jed said, "Come on." He continued to smile, and he looked right into her eyes. "Let's see if you can stand up." He held out his hand.

Adora took it. He had never removed the fingerless black gloves, so all at once her hand was engulfed in leather and heat. Her whole body seemed to tingle, from the moist skin at her hairline to the pink-enameled toes inside her pink tennis shoes. With a small groan at the effort, she stood.

"Okay?" he asked softly.

She coughed—and ordered herself to pull it together. "Sure. Fine, just fine."

He released her hand. Smiling like an idiot, she brushed off the back of her shorts. He gestured for her to take the lead, so she did.

They started down the trail. Right away she wished she'd let him go first. Her bottom felt numb, and her insides quivered like jelly. It took all the concentration she could muster to walk with some degree of dignity.

They went on as before, not saying anything. And with the silence between them, the wild sounds all around seemed suddenly magnified. From the rude call of a mockingbird to the croaking of the creek frogs, every sound had a sensual intent. Even the buzzing of the honeybees that swarmed the blackberry bushes on either side of the trail struck her as louder, more intense somehow.

Which was ridiculous. The bees were not buzzing any louder than before. It was just her imagination. And nothing had happened between her and Jed Ryder. She'd fallen on the trail and he'd helped her to her feet. End of story.

Now they would find Lola and go their separate ways. And the next time she saw him, she'd smile politely, say hello and walk on by.

The path had leveled out, and they were very near the creek. Then they rounded a sharp bend in the trail. It took Adora a minute to realize what she saw on the ground ahead of her. A woman lay there, on her back, in the arching shadow of a birch tree.

It was Lola.

Two

She lay faceup, with her eyes closed. Adora thought that she looked peaceful, except for the bloodless pallor of her skin. A dented tin pail had rolled a few feet away from her, spilling a shiny trail of blackberries out across the ground.

"God. Ma..." The gentle voice wasn't much above a whisper, but Adora's heart stopped at the anguish in it.

He shoved around her, ran to Lola, dropped to his knees at her side. "Ma..." Frantically he felt for a pulse. "Ma. Come on, Ma..." He tipped her head back, checked beyond her pale lips for any obstruction and then began to breath into her mouth.

Adora stood rooted to the spot, feeling outside her own body somehow. As if she weren't really there. As if the desperate man kneeling on the ground wasn't Jed

Ryder. And the still form of the woman wasn't anyone she knew.

Because that pale, lifeless figure just couldn't be Lola. Not Lola, who worked for her. Lola, with her scratchy voice and dry sense of humor. Lola, who took care of all the older ladies on Senior Citizen Discount Day, who was so funny and patient with them, giving them the same boring cuts every time and never getting fed up because they wouldn't even spring for a set or a blow-dry.

Jed looked up at her. Now he was calm. A terrible calm.

"Jed?" she asked, hoping for reassurance, hoping he would tell her that Lola wasn't really dead.

"Get help," he said in a whisper that rang in her ears like a shout. "Run like hell."

And she did. She turned and ran back the way they'd come. She tore along that trail, shoving branches aside, scrambling upward when the trail climbed, half sliding, half running when the trail cut downhill. Each breath burned in her lungs, and her blood pounded so loud through her body that she could hear nothing else. She stumbled often but somehow managed to keep herself from actually falling.

The going got easier once she staggered up the bank that led to the bridge. From there, she ran on pavement, which wasn't nearly as tough as running on the rocky, uneven trail. She tore down the street as fast as her shaking legs would carry her, her heart working so hard it felt as if it might explode in her chest.

Tilly Simpson, who worked as Doc Mott's assistant, nurse and EMT combined, was standing behind the little counter on one side of the waiting room when Adora burst in the door of the clinic.

Tilly's mouth dropped open.

Adora pressed a hand to her side, gulping for breath, noticing distantly that there were no patients waiting. The big clock on the fake-wood-paneled wall between the two Norman Rockwell prints said it was 2:39.

Tilly started sputtering. "Adora, what—?"

"It's Lola," Adora got out between starving gulps for air, "Lola Pierce. Down the Trout Creek Trail. Oh Tilly, I think she's dead."

They allowed Adora to ride in the ambulance, a very short ride, down the street and around the corner with the siren blaring. And then they let her carry the light-weight, roll-up stretcher, since both the doctor and Tilly had plenty to carry themselves. They tore down the bank to creekside as fast as they could go. But they weren't more than a few hundred yards along the trail when Jed came loping toward them with Lola's lifeless body cradled in his arms—and desolation in his eyes.

A few minutes later, right there on the trail, Doc Mott pronounced Lola dead. He looked at Jed with weary regret. "It was a stroke, I think. Or possibly a heart attack. There'll be an autopsy. And then we can be sure."

Jed said nothing, only nodded. They'd already laid Lola on the stretcher. Doc Mott took one end, and Jed took the other.

A small crowd had gathered near the ambulance when Jed and Doc Mott reached the top of the bank. Carefully, the two men hoisted their unmoving burden over the low railing onto the bridge. Adora and Tilly followed close behind, laden with the equipment that, in the end, had been of no use.

"Stand back, folks," Doc Mott said, as they put Lola

on the cot in the back of the ambulance. "Please, folks. Stand back."

Adora could hear them whispering.

"It's Lola. Lola Pierce."

"Gone?"

"Yeah, it sure looks like it."

Deputy Don Peebles, whom Adora had known since grade school, had just emerged from his big, sheriff's office four-by-four. "What's the story here, Doc?"

"Lola Pierce has died."

"Of what?"

"I can't say for sure at this point. Looks like a stroke or a heart attack. The autopsy will tell us more." Doc Mott closed the double doors on Lola's still form.

"Who found the body?"

"Jed here." Doc Mott nodded in Jed's direction. "And Adora Beaudine."

Don turned to Jed. "I'll have a few questions for you, Ryder." He looked for and found Adora. "And you too, Dory."

"You can ask your questions later," Jed said. "I gotta get to my sister."

"I'll ask my questions *now*." Don spoke in a tone of unyielding authority.

Adora stepped up. "Can you make it quick, Don? Please? Tiff's only eleven. Jed should be with her."

Don shook his head. "I've got a job to do, Dory. Now both of you just move over there, beside my vehicle."

Adora glanced at Jed, whose jaw seemed set in concrete; he looked as if he had no intention of following Deputy Don's orders. *Just what he needs right now,* she thought grimly. *To get in trouble with the law.*

"Come on, Jed," she coaxed.

He didn't budge. So she grabbed his huge, hard arm and pulled on it until he went with her to where Don had pointed.

The deputy was already turning, assuming responsibility for crowd control. "All right now, folks. You'll have to step away from the ambulance. Tilly's ready to move out." He gave a quick salute to Tilly as she climbed into the cab on the driver's side.

Doc Mott came over to Jed and Adora. He spoke quietly to Jed. "We'll be taking your mom back to the clinic. From there, she'll go to Reno, where the Washoe County Coroner will handle the autopsy. The whole procedure could take anywhere from twenty-four hours to a few days. You'll want to have chosen a funeral home by the time they release the body."

"Okay."

The doc glanced toward the ambulance where Tilly was waiting for him, and then turned back to Jed. "Folks in town know you treated your mom right, Jed. And it is important that you be with your sister now. I'll tell Don to make it snappy."

"Thanks," Jed muttered.

"No problem." After sharing a few quiet words with the deputy, Doc Mott got in the ambulance, and Tilly carefully steered it out onto the small bridge. Moments later, the big white van disappeared, turning left onto Buckland Avenue, headed back to the clinic.

Don instructed Adora to wait several yards away while he talked to Jed. And then he wouldn't let Jed go until he'd heard Adora's side of the story. He did make it reasonably quick, though. Within ten minutes of asking the first question, he was nodding at Jed, who leaned against the bridge railing, muscular arms crossed over his powerful chest, looking impatient and more dangerous than usual.

"Okay, you can go," Don said. "You'll be hearing from me again, as soon as we get the autopsy results."

Jed dropped his crossed arms and straightened from the railing. Without a word he headed for home.

The crowd was breaking up, but the folks who still hung around watched Jed as he strode past them. Adora could see the sympathy in their eyes. But none of them said anything; none of them reached out. He was wild Jed Ryder, after all. And who could say what he might do?

Lizzie Spooner, who'd shown up a few minutes before and had been waiting patiently for Don to finish with Adora, now moved to her side. "You okay?"

Adora blinked and looked at her friend.

Lizzie frowned. "You look bad. Come on. I'll take you back to your place. I was just over there, looking for you. I signed for a package. From your mother. A present, I'll bet. Let's go and—"

Jed was almost at the turn to Bridge Street by then. Adora realized she couldn't just let him go. "Jed!"

Jed stopped. He turned. He hadn't put those shades back on after she'd fallen on the trail, so she was able to meet his eyes. She saw willingness in them. If she wanted to go with him, to be there when he broke the awful news to Tiff, it was okay with him.

"Wait up!" she called. She felt Lizzie's hand clutching her arm. She brushed it off. "Gotta go."

"But, Dory...."

"I'll call you."

"I left the package on the back step."

"Thanks. Later, really." And she took off at a run.

Jed waited, but only until she caught up with him. And then he was moving again, walking fast.

"I want to get my bike." They had reached the corner of Church and Bridge. "You go on over to the house."

"Should I go in without you?"

He cast her a grim smile. "Walk slow. And I'll beat you there."

"Okay."

He took off at a dead run. Adora turned the corner onto Church Street, walking slowly, as Jed had told her to, thinking about Tiffany, who was waiting for her mother to come home.

Jed parked his bike in the attached garage and he and Adora entered the trim wood frame cottage through the kitchen.

They went straight to the living room. There, the first thing Adora noticed was the scent of spiced apple potpourri. She spotted the source: a green glass bowl on a side table, filled with the stuff. Adora had made that potpourri herself.

And Lola had loved it. "It's autumn and apple pie and my grandma huggin' me, all just from a smell," she had declared.

So of course Adora had given her some.

But she would never give her any again.

Blinking back tears, Adora looked around the tidy room, at silk freesias in a dimestore vase on a cheap veneer coffee table. At *People* magazines and *Ladies' Home Journals* arranged in a fan. At the two slightly threadbare flowered easy chairs and the tan velour couch.

Tiff was asleep on that couch, curled up on her side,

with one hand under her head and the other pressed against her heart. Her silky auburn hair, which Adora had cut into a cute little wedge for her, lay smooth and straight against her soft cheek. She was smiling a little, as if her dreams were sweet ones.

Looking at her, Adora just wanted to let her go right on sleeping. She glanced at Jed and thought he felt the same.

But then, as if she'd sensed them watching her, Tiff opened her eyes. For a moment she seemed dazed. Then her eyes cleared and her sleepy smile grew wider. She sat up and yawned.

"What's up, guys?" She looked from Adora to her brother and back again. And her smile faded. Worry clouded her dark eyes. "What?"

Jed dropped to the couch beside her and wrapped one of those huge arms around her. "Tiff…" And that was all he seemed to be able to say.

Tiff nudged her shoulder against him, fond and impatient at the same time. "*What?*" She looked at Adora for an answer. "Dory, come on…"

Adora prayed for the right words to come to her.

Before they did, Jed said, "It's Ma."

Tiff turned to him. "Mom?"

Jed nodded.

Tiff worried her lower lip. "I don't…um. What do you mean?"

Jed started to speak.

But before he could get a word out, Tiff went on, "It's weird. I was just dreaming about Mom. She hugged me. She said never to forget how much she loves me. That's kind of funny, huh? Like I could forget something like that. You know how she is, always grabbing me and kissin' on me and saying I'm her precious baby girl. She looked…really peaceful in my dream. But her skin was too white, you know?"

Adora remembered Lola lying on the trail. Peaceful. And pale…

"Jed?" Tiff nudged him again. "Jed. What's the matter?"

And somehow, he said it. "Tiff, something happened. Ma was picking berries. Down by Trout Creek. She had…a heart attack, or something. We're not sure."

Tiffany shook her head, her hair fanning out, then falling so prettily against her cheek. "A heart attack? Mom? No. There's nothing wrong with Mom. Mom is fine. Mom is—" She ran out of words. She turned to Adora, her big brown eyes filling, her face going red. "Dory. Dory, what is he saying?"

Adora gulped, feeling answering tears rising, willing them down. "She's gone, honey."

Tiffany gulped in a breath. And then she let it out on a tight little moan. "No…"

Jed rubbed his eyes. "Aw, Tiff…"

Tiffany turned to him again, her soft lips quivering, but her chin held high. "Gone. You mean…dead?"

Jed only nodded.

"Mom?" she whispered. "Mom's dead.…"

And then, with a cry, she flung herself against her brother. She grabbed a handful of his black vest in each of her small fists, and she pressed her face against him, at that shining silver cross. "No," she said softly.

"Yeah," Jed whispered back.

"No!"

This time, Jed said nothing.

But Tiffany couldn't stop. "No," she said. "No, no, no, no…" over and over, as if by saying it so many times, she might bring Lola back.

Soon enough, the nos became sobs. And the tears spilled over.

Adora stood there, feeling useless, aching for both of them, as Tiffany cried and Jed held her, rocking her like a baby, stroking the smooth red-brown cap of her hair.

Finally, Tiff calmed a little. She pulled away from Jed. Adora spotted a box of tissues on a side table. She went and got it. Tiff took a handful. She dried her eyes and blew her nose, hiccupping a little, trying to bear up.

Watching her, Adora couldn't help recalling her own foolish, self-indulgent tears earlier that afternoon and feeling that her own problems weren't much at all compared to this. She also wondered about the precious minutes she'd kept Jed in her apartment, listening to her woes and drinking champagne. Could those minutes have made a difference? If she'd told Jed right away about where Lola had gone, might they have found her in time to save her life?

Tiff blew her nose for the third time, then scooted over closer to Jed and patted the space where she'd been. "Sit by us, Dory. Please."

Adora pushed her guilty thoughts away. Now wasn't the time to ponder them. She sat next to Tiff. With a torn little sigh, Tiff leaned against her for a moment. Then she leaned the other way, against Jed, who wrapped an arm around her and rested his bearded chin on the crown of her head.

"What happened?" Tiff asked. And a sob escaped her. She pressed the back of her hand to her mouth, composing herself. Then she took a deep breath. "Please tell me. I want to know."

Without going into too much detail, they told the sad story. Jed was explaining that it would be a day or two before they knew for sure why Lola had died, when they heard footsteps on the front walk. The curtains of the front window were open. From where he sat, Jed could see the porch and the steps leading up to it. He glanced out—and swore low, with feeling.

Tiff stared up at him. "Who is it?" She turned to look out the window, then moaned. "Oh, no."

Adora turned to see, but the angle was wrong. Whoever it was had moved out of her line of vision and stood right at the door. The visitor knocked.

Jed pulled his sister just a little closer to his side and caught Adora's eye. "Answer it, will you?"

"No!" Tiff sounded childish, even petulant suddenly, not at all like the incredibly gallant girl who had asked so bravely to be told how her mother had died.

But Jed was nodding grimly. "We'll have to deal with her eventually. There's no sense in trying to pretend we won't."

Tiff sniffed in outrage and whirled on Jed. "But—"

"Shh." He smoothed her hair, then looked at Adora. "Go ahead. Please."

Adora got up and pulled open the door.

On the porch stood Charity Laidlaw, who was Tiffany's aunt—as well as the woman who had once accused Jed of rape.

Three

Behind Charity and off to the side a little stood her husband Morton, looking miserable.

Charity spoke first, which was no surprise to anyone.

"Hello, Adora." Even in greeting, her tone left no room for compromise.

"Hello, Mrs. Laidlaw."

It was odd, Adora thought. Charity had nice, even features, cornflower blue eyes and ash blond hair that curled softly around her face. She'd kept her figure slim. She should have been attractive. But she wasn't. She was too self-righteous to be good-looking.

"May we come in?"

Adora glanced at Jed, giving him one more chance to change his mind. But Jed only nodded. So Adora stepped back and pushed open the screen.

"We've heard the terrible news," Charity intoned as she entered, followed at a respectful distance by her browbeaten spouse. "And we've come to take our poor niece home with us." Charity caught sight of Jed right then. Her finely cut nostrils flared, as if she smelled something bad.

Jed and Tiff stood as one.

"Tiff *is* home, Charity." Jed seemed to take pleasure in calling Tiff's aunt by her given name, which few, if any, in Red Dog City ever dared to do. "And I'm here, so I'll take care of her."

One corner of Charity's pretty upper lip lifted a fraction, in a sort of well-bred snarl. "That is the most absurd suggestion I have ever heard."

"It's not a suggestion. It's a fact."

Charity looked at Tiff, her expression turning marginally kinder. "Tiffany. Dear—"

Tiff hunched closer to Jed. "I'm staying here, with my brother."

Charity emitted a harumph of impatience. "But that's impossible, dear. Your brother lives out in the woods in that primitive cabin of his. And questionable men work for him. He's not set up to care for an impressionable young girl."

"We'll manage, Charity." Jed's tone was deceptively gentle, as always. But his eyes gave away his true feelings. They were twin points of dry ice. "I've got my own room here, over the garage. I'll move in there fulltime. It can all be worked out."

Charity drew her shoulders back so far it was a surprise she didn't fall over backward. And when she spoke, it was with great care, as if she were putting everything she had into her effort to remain civil. "But you're gone all day. The child will run wild."

Tiff jumped in, insulted. "I don't run wild."

Charity sighed. "Now, Tiffany, I know how upset you are and I—"

"No. No, you don't. You don't know anything. You're a mean, old—"

Jed coughed and gave Tiff's shoulder a squeeze. Tiff fell silent.

Charity drove her point home. "You cannot be alone all day long, and that is that."

Tiff looked up at Jed, pleading with her eyes. But Jed said nothing. Adora knew what he must be thinking: that it wouldn't be right for Tiff to go completely unsupervised all day, every day. It was a problem, one to which he had no immediate solution.

But Adora did. "Look. I'm just around the corner. I can keep an eye on Tiff during the day, the same as Lola did, from the shop."

Charity drew in a sharp, indignant breath and focused her narrowed eyes on Adora. If looks could do harm, Adora would have needed medical attention on the spot.

Tiffany crowed in triumph. "See? Dory will help." She looked up at her brother, her eyes full of fevered hope. "I'll be with *you*, won't I, Jed?"

He gave her shoulder another squeeze. "Damn straight. We're family."

Charity would not give up. "I beg your pardon. I'm every bit as much a part of Tiffany's family as you are. And Morton and I are much more suitable as substitute parents than you'll ever be."

Jed didn't waver. "Look, Charity. Tiff wants to be with me. And I can take care of her. And with Adora helping out, we'll get along just fine."

Charity glared at him long and hard, trying to break him with a look. It didn't work. So she brought out the big guns.

"Let's be frank here, Jed Ryder. You aren't fit to raise a child."

Tiff let out an angry cry. Jed soothed her. "Shh..." Then he met Charity's venomous glare once more and advised, softly as always, "Don't go too far."

Charity's nostrils had gone dead white. She sucked in a big breath through them and then announced sanctimoniously, "I most certainly *will* go too far. I'll go as far as I have to go."

Morton, looking anxious, actually stepped forward. "Charity, maybe we—"

Charity shot a murderous glance his way. "Shut up, Morton. This has to be said." She rounded on Jed once more, her lip curling in disgust. "It's an absolute outrage, Jedediah Ryder, that you could even imagine you'd be allowed to take care of my brother's child. I'm warning you now—"

But Jed had heard enough. "That's it. Get out."

Charity barreled right on. "I will not stand by and let you ruin that child's life."

Jed took one step forward. "I said get out."

Charity sneered. "You are a rude creature. A disgusting, irresponsible—"

Morton scooted between Charity and Jed and grabbed his wife's arm. "Charity. We've been asked to leave."

"Don't touch me." She slapped at his hands. "We have a duty to my brother's child."

Jed was through talking. He advanced on Charity.

She gasped, whirled and fled to the door, Morton at her heels. Once there, she couldn't resist a parting shot. "This isn't the end of it."

Morton shooed her over the threshold and pushed her down the steps and along the walk. Adora slid forward and shut the door, resting her forehead against it once it was closed, thinking that she had never in her life been so relieved to see anybody go.

"Thanks." It was Jed's voice.

Adora turned to meet those cloud-colored eyes and felt warm all over at the pure gratitude she saw in them. "Hey, what are friends for?"

Tiffany looked up at Jed. "I don't want to go with her. I couldn't *stand* to go with her. She always treated Mom like she wasn't good enough to be married to her precious brother. And she doesn't really even care about me, I know it. She only cares that you and me don't get to stay together."

Jed shook his head. "There's nothing she can do."

"But she said—"

He waved her fears away. "Don't stew about it, Tiff. With Adora looking out for you during the day, we've got it covered. Charity's threats are empty ones, I promise you."

"Are you sure?"

"I'm dead positive. Now, we have enough to worry about as it is. So let's forget about your Aunt Charity."

Tiff closed her eyes and sighed. "I hope you're right."

"I am right. Stop worrying."

Though no one felt much like eating, Adora stayed to cook dinner. As she put together the simple meal, friends and neighbors started calling to offer condolences and aid. Adora handled most of those calls, soothing people, telling them briefly how Lola had died and promising to call them back if there was anything at all that they could do.

After the dishes were cleaned up, Jed, Tiffany and Adora wandered into the living room. Jed and Tiff sat on the couch, and Adora took one of the easy chairs. They began to talk about Lola, remembering the best things about her: her laugh, her generous heart, how sensitive she'd always been to the way other people felt. Tiff and Adora cried some, as they all tried to deal with the fact that someone who had been so much alive that morning was now gone for good.

"I still feel like she can't be gone," Tiff admitted.

"Me too," Adora agreed. "It seems like any minute she's going to walk in that door."

It was well after dark when Tiff rose from the couch. "I think I'll just go on to bed now."

Adora pushed herself out of the easy chair and held out her arms. Tiff ran to her.

"I'm glad you were here," Tiff whispered as she hugged Adora close.

"Me, too." She cupped Tiff's sweet face in her hands and looked into those soft, dark eyes. "I'm going home now." Gently she smoothed Tiff's silky hair. "But I'll be back in the morning, to fix you some breakfast. Okay?"

"Mmm-hmm."

Once Tiff had disappeared down the tiny central hall, Jed walked out to the porch with Adora. They stood for a few moments, there in the darkness, listening to the crickets and one lonesome frog croaking forlornly somewhere out on the lawn. Eventually Adora felt Jed's pale gaze on her and turned enough to give him a smile.

He asked, "Do you think I did the right thing?"

She leaned against one of the four posts that held up the porch roof. "Deciding to keep Tiff with you, you mean?"

"Yeah."

She thought of the Laidlaws, of their settled, middle-class life. They'd already raised two daughters, so it was a job they were familiar with. And Morton was a nice enough man, a retired dentist who had closed his practice in nearby Portola just a few years ago. Adora and her family, like most folks in Red Dog City, had always gone to Doctor Laidlaw when they needed dental work. He knew how to administer a shot of novocaine so you barely felt it.

Jed was chuckling. "Don't answer. I can tell by your face."

She wrinkled her nose at him. "What?"

"You have your doubts about me."

"Actually, I was thinking about Morton Laidlaw. That he's a nice man, even if he is married to Charity." She grinned. "You know what Reggie Kratt says about him?" Ancient Reggie Kratt ran Kratt's Hardware, over on Commercial Row.

Jed knew. He put on a voice like Reggie's. "'That man is more than hen*pecked.* He's hen*hammered,* and it's a cryin' shame.'"

Adora laughed, and Jed did, too.

Then they fell silent. That frog started croaking again. Jed hitched a leg onto the porch rail. "So why did you volunteer to help me out?"

She looked out toward the street. "I don't know, exactly."

"Yeah, you do."

"Well..."

"Tell it like it is."

She met his eyes again. "Tiff wants to be with you."

"And?"

"There's more to raising a child than being respectable."

"Good. 'Cause most people would say I come up zero in that department."

"Charity's…well, I'd hate to have to live with her."

"And?"

She sought the right words, but didn't find them.

He urged her on. "Spill it."

"Charity reminds me of my mother." It was out before Adora really considered how it would sound. She hastened to amend, "I mean, one side of my mother. The side that thinks she has to control everything. The side that's always worried about what other people will think." Adora looked out at the stars. The moon was no more than a sliver. It hung high above them, looking very far away.

She could feel Jed watching her. And when he spoke, she could hear the smile in his voice. "Are you a secret rebel, Adora Beaudine?"

She made a scoffing sound. "No way. You ought to know that, after the things I told you today." Lord, was that only a few hours ago? It seemed like years, somehow.

He grunted. "Right. You wanna get married. To a guy in a Brooks Brothers suit."

She had a silly urge to argue the point. But why? "You're right. A guy in a Brooks Brothers suit is exactly what I want."

"Still, I know you went with Dillon McKenna. Back in high school, when his reputation was almost as bad as mine."

She kept her eyes on the faraway moon. "That was different. We were only kids. A crush. And in case you haven't heard, Dillon's married to my sister Cat now."

"I heard."

Adora thought about Dillon. Like Jed, he'd left town

when he was barely grown. He'd returned to Red Dog City just last winter, an international celebrity whose career as a professional daredevil had ended after one of his jumps almost killed him. As soon as he'd set eyes on Cat again, he'd known what he wanted. Cat had taken some convincing. But in the end, Dillon had been more than persuasive enough to win her.

"Jealous?" Somehow, Jed made the question sound tender.

Adora looked at him then. "Of what?"

"That your first love belongs to your sister now?"

She stared at him, wondering how he managed to ask her such personal questions—and yet not offend her at all when he did it. And he'd hit right on the mark, too. She had been jealous. At first. There had been trouble between her and Cat. But it had all worked out in the end. Now Adora couldn't picture Dillon with anyone but Cat.

She said, "No, I'm not jealous. And if I was, I'd be suffering for nothing. No other woman's got a chance with Dillon. He's crazy over Cat. And she's nuts for him. They're so in love, it's embarrassing sometimes to be in the same room with them. They forget other people exist."

The porch light caught on the diamond stud in Jed's ear, making it glitter. "You wanna be loved like that?" His voice, always low, was lower than ever. And intimate.

She couldn't help thinking of that afternoon, on the trail by Trout Creek. Of the impossible way she had felt then. Of the way she felt right now...

"Come on. Say it out straight."

She gulped, and then she did it; she said it out

straight. "Yeah. I do. I want to be loved like that. What woman wouldn't?"

He grinned, white teeth flashing. The diamond stud gleamed. Right then he looked like a pirate from one of those old movies that Cat used to take her to when they were kids. "You think Mr. Brooks Brothers Suit is gonna love you like that?"

She slid around the porch post, away from him a little. "I, um..."

"You said you try too hard. You said you scare men away."

"Yes, I—"

"I gotta tell you. I keep lookin' for a woman who'll try hard *enough*."

Adora had no idea what to say to that. He'd taken off those black fingerless gloves some time before dinner, and now she found herself looking at his hands. They were big, rough-looking hands. But they had been so gentle, soothing Tiff.

He was staring down at his heavy black boots. "Am I outta line?"

Her throat felt like someone was squeezing it. She had to cough to open it up. "A little, yes."

He shrugged, a lazy raising of those big, thick shoulders. Then he looked up from his boots and into her eyes. "Sorry."

"It's okay." She glanced out toward the street. "I really should go."

"I know." A half smile curved his lips, but his eyes seemed far away and sad. Adora knew he must be thinking of Lola again. "Thanks. For everything."

"I'll be back. In the morning. Early."

"Good enough."

She slid around the post, toward the front walk this

time. Swiftly she ran down the steps and out to the street. She sensed that he watched after her, until the trees that lined the road blocked his view. But she never once turned back to see if what she sensed was really true.

At home Adora put the package from her mother aside long enough to play her messages back. There were quite a few. Each of her sisters had called, to wish her a happy birthday. And Lizzie had called twice.

"Call me back the minute you get in," Lizzie's recorded voice commanded.

Bobby Tamberlaine, who'd been a pal of Adora's since they were both in first grade, had left a message, too. "I heard about Lola." His kind voice held real sympathy. "Just wanted you to know I'm here if you need me."

Making a mental note to call Lizzie before she went to bed, Adora took a moment to toss the empty champagne bottle in the trash and to wash out the champagne flutes with which she and Jed had toasted her birthday. She smiled ruefully, remembering how she'd planned to smash them when the champagne was gone. Somehow, that idea seemed utterly silly now.

So she dried them with care. And found herself thinking what might have been—if only she hadn't dragged Jed into her apartment, if only she'd sent him off for the trail by Trout Creek right away, if only...

Adora put the glasses in the cupboard and closed the door. There was no point in dwelling on it. Not now, anyway. She would wait for the autopsy. And if she learned that a few minutes might have made a difference, well, she'd have to deal with that when the time came.

Resolutely, she turned to the package from her mother. Inside were two brightly wrapped gifts. Adora chose the smaller one to open first. It contained a single strand of pearls.

Sighing, she lifted the strand from its velvet case. The necklace had once belonged to her grandmother, and Adora had always admired it.

She bit her lower lip, feeling remorseful. Her mother had sent her such a beautiful gift—and Adora had paid her back by comparing her to cold, self-righteous Charity Laidlaw.

What had gone wrong between herself and her mother?

None of her sisters had trouble getting along with Lottie. But Lottie drove Adora nuts. And why was that? After all, both she and her mother wanted the same thing: a husband for Adora. But it wasn't happening. And as each new man came and went, Lottie grew more and more insistent on advising Adora about her love life. And Adora became more and more fed up with listening to that advice.

She should appreciate her mother more. The loss of Lola, which sent a fresh pulse of grief through her every time she thought of it, made it all so clear. Life was short. Too short to waste time holding resentments against people you loved.

Adora laid the pearls back in their case. "I'm sorry, Mom," she whispered aloud, though there was no one there to hear. "I'll be more patient with you, I promise."

But then she opened the other gift. It was a book. A self-help book: *Desperate Women and the Men Who Keep Leaving Them.*

"Are you a Desperate Woman?" the jacket blurb inquired in bold text. "Take the Desperate Woman test. Learn about the Ten Fatal Love Traps that keep you from finding the happiness and love you deserve. You'll discover how to spot the real Mr. Right and stop fooling around with that seductive, but completely destructive, Mr. Wrong.

"Change your life. Starting today. With the wisdom you'll find waiting in the pages of *Desperate Women and the Men Who Keep Leaving Them.*"

The phone rang just after Adora threw the book across the room.

Adora knew who it would be. And it was.

"Do you like the necklace, honey?"

She focused with grim determination on being appreciative. "You know I do. I've loved those pearls since I was little and you used to wear them to church. Thanks, Mom."

"You're very welcome. I've always meant that those pearls would be yours. And, by the way, I've heard that that book is excellent."

"I'll bet it is."

"Are you all right? You sound strained."

"I'm just fine, Mom." She thought of Lola again. "But I have some sad news, I'm afraid."

"Oh, dear. What's happened?"

For what seemed like the hundredth time that day, Adora explained that Lola Pierce had died, then went on to tell her mother how she planned to do all she could for Lola's family during the tough days that would be coming up.

Lottie listened and clucked her tongue sympathetically. "Lola was a sweet woman, I always thought."

"Yes, she was."

"And that poor child. Tiffany is her name, right?"

"Yes. Tiffany."

"How old is the poor thing?"

"Eleven."

Lottie clucked her tongue some more. "Of course, Bob and I will send flowers. Which funeral home is it?"

"I'll let you know as soon as Jed decides."

There was a tiny pause. "Jed? Jed Ryder, you mean?"

"Yes, Mom," Adora gritted her teeth. "Lola was his mother. Remember?"

"Of course I remember. But I just—"

"What?"

"Are you upset?"

"No."

"Well, you certainly sound upset."

"It's been a tough day."

"Oh, honey. I'm sure it has."

"You just *what?*"

"Pardon me?"

"You were talking about Jed, Mom. You said, 'But I just—' and then you didn't finish."

"Well, you interrupted me."

Mentally, Adora counted to ten.

"Adora?"

"Mother, just tell me what you were going to say about Jed."

"Oh. Well, it was only… Didn't he leave town years and years ago, after that horrible incident with Dawn Laidlaw?"

"Yes, he did. But he came back. Right around the time you married Bob and moved to Tucson."

"Oh, yes. I remember now. He had become a…a biker sort of man, as I recall."

"Mother. Jed is a *terrific* sort of man."

"Well, I—"

"Let me finish. Lemuel Pierce died of cancer, do you remember that?"

"Of course."

"It was a very long, painful death. And very expensive. By the time he was gone, Lola and Tiff had nothing left. But then Jed came back. He bought a house for them to live in. And Lola told me herself that whenever she came up short, he would help pay the bills. He's done a lot, to take care of them. And now that Lola's gone, he's going to take care of Tiffany."

"Oh, my. Is that appropriate?"

"What do you mean?"

"Well, it's obvious, isn't it? An eleven-year-old girl. And a *biker* man."

"He's her *brother*. And, yes, he rides a Harley. But he also has a business of his own. He makes a good living."

"Doing what?"

"He has a machine shop. He machines custom parts for vintage airplanes. Lola told me that he gets most of his contacts through the big air shows in Reno. Really, he's quite responsible. And I told you, I'll be helping out."

That caused dead silence on the line. Then Lottie carefully inquired, "Exactly how will you be helping out?"

"I'll keep an eye on Tiff during the day, while Jed's at work."

More silence, then, "But honey, what about your own life?"

Adora had the sudden urge to cry out, *What about my life, Mother? What about my boring, empty,* loveless *life?* But somehow, she held that cry back. And right at that moment she heard a double click on the line.

Saved by call waiting, she thought. "I'm going to help out, Mom. Get used to it. And now, I have another call."

"But, Adora—"

"Really. I have to go. I love you. And thanks for the pearls."

"Just stay away from—"

Adora cut her mother off before she could say Jed's name.

The other caller was Lizzie. She wanted to hear all about Lola. So Adora told the story all over again.

"And how's Tiffany?" Lizzie asked.

Adora told her how brave Tiff had been.

"What will happen to her now?" Lizzie wondered aloud.

"Jed will take care of her. And I'm going to help." It came out sounding defiant—and Adora didn't care.

Lizzie didn't argue, only asked warily, "Won't Charity Laidlaw have something to say about that?"

Adora admitted that Charity had already been to Lola's trying to take Tiff away. "But Tiff wants to be with Jed. And Jed wants to take care of her."

"Then he should get in to see Wanda."

Adora wrapped the phone cord around her index finger. "I didn't even think about that." Wanda Spooner was Lizzie's sister-in-law and the local representative for Child Protective Services.

"Well, you should think about it," Lizzie said. "He needs to file for guardianship right away. If I were him, I'd show up at the Department of Social Services in Quincy at nine sharp tomorrow morning."

"You're right. I'll get ahold of Jed and tell him right now."

She hung up and called Jed.

"I'll head over there tomorrow first thing," he promised. And then he told her how great she was to be looking out for him and Tiff.

Adora felt a glow all through herself at his praise. She made a few modest noises, then said goodbye.

Then as soon as she hung up, she started thinking about Jed's appearance. Really, he should look low-key and well-groomed for that visit with Wanda. He needed something different to wear than a T-shirt with the sleeves torn off and old, beat-up jeans....

Four

Adora arrived at the house on Church Street before seven the next morning, so she already had breakfast well underway when Jed came down from his room over the garage. She heard the side door open and turned from pouring pancakes on the griddle. And there he was, big and wild looking as ever.

He must have just had his shower because his hair hung in wet black coils around his shoulders, making water spots on the rumpled dark blue T-shirt he wore, a T-shirt from which the sleeves had been torn off. Did he own a shirt that still had sleeves? Adora was beginning to doubt it. His blue jeans were stained, creased and faded. They clung lovingly to his lean, hard legs. Beyond that, they actually seemed to cup and display his—

"Mornin'."

She shifted her glance from where it had no business

being and met his silvery eyes. A smile flirted with the corners of his mouth. Had he noticed where she'd been looking? She didn't want to know.

"Good morning." It came out sounding squeaky. She ordered her silly face not to blush. "Try those on." She pointed with her spatula in the direction of the clothes she'd laid over a chair, then turned back to the pancakes, which were just about ready to flip.

He wore moccasins instead of the usual big, black boots, so his feet made no sound as he stalked over and scooped up the blue chambray shirt and chinos. From the corner of her eye, she watched him look the clothes over. His lip had curled in disgust by the time he threw them down again.

"Straight clothes. What the hell is this?"

Tiffany, who'd come to the table with red, puffy eyes and had only been pretending to eat her pancakes, actually stifled a giggle at the outrage in her brother's voice. Jed turned his glare her way. She wiped the smirk from her face and got busy on her breakfast.

Jed demanded, "Whose clothes are these?"

"Bobby Tamberlaine's." Bobby was not only Adora's buddy, he stood six-one and lifted weights in his spare time. Jed was bigger than Bobby, but not that much bigger. Adora felt reasonably sure the clothes would fit. "I stopped by his house last night and borrowed them, after I called you about going to Quincy this morning."

"I don't wear straight clothes."

Adora flipped the last pancake, turned from the stove once more and gave him a perky smile. "Today you do. Today, a good impression could be very important." She set down the spatula and folded her arms over her chest, to show she meant business. "Now, come on. It's not as if it was a *suit* or anything."

He made a growly sort of noise. "You'd love that, wouldn't you? To get me into a suit?"

She kept her determined stance and her perky smile as she trilled out sweetly, "Your pancakes will burn."

He went on glaring. "Mind if I eat first?"

"Of course not." She turned back to the stove. "Have a seat."

After he ate, he left for his room again, only to emerge a few minutes later wearing the slacks and shirt. The shirt strained at the shoulder seams and the pants were a tad short. But altogether, he didn't look bad. He had tied his hair back with a strip of leather, and while he still wore the silver cross, he'd actually removed the diamond stud that usually glinted in his ear.

"Well?" He gazed at her defiantly.

She nodded her approval. "It'll pass."

He muttered, "Next you'll be wantin' me to shave my beard and cut my hair."

"Actually, the beard is quite attractive. And your hair looks fine tied back."

"Whoa. Major praise."

She noted that he'd switched the moccasins for his black boots. They didn't work at all with the pale blue shirt and tan pants. "Bobby's feet are smaller than yours. I could tell just by eyeing them. So I didn't even bother to try to borrow shoes from him." She looked up into his face again. "Do you have anything but those boots? Even tennis shoes would do."

He grunted. "I think I tossed a pair of old cowhide Acmes in the back of the closet a year or two ago."

"Acmes. As in cowboy boots? *Tan* cowboy boots?"

"Right on."

"The boots are here? In your room over the garage?"

"You got it."

"Get them."

He trudged out to his room for the second time and came back wearing the tan boots. They were a little beat up, and down at the heels, but still a big improvement over the black ones.

"Can I go now?" His expression said she'd better not try to change one more thing about the way he looked. "I want to run out to my shop before I head over to Quincy. I gotta check on the men. See that they're handling everything all right." Adora knew that he hired other bikers, semioutlaws like himself. She had run into a few of them over the past couple of years and thus could understand why he wanted to check on them.

"Good luck in Quincy," she said brightly. "We'll be right here when you get back."

He frowned. "What about *your* shop?"

"I'll be closed for the day."

"That's not right. You're great to help out. But I don't want it wreckin' your business."

"It will not wreck my business. All my ladies knew Lola. And loved her. It would be in bad taste to be open today."

"But—"

"Don't argue with me, Jed Ryder. I know what I'm doing. And you need to get going. You said so yourself."

He put up both hands. "Okay, okay."

"Now *out*."

"Yes, ma'am." He turned and left through the kitchen again. A few moments later, she heard the loud roar of his bike starting up. Then she went to look for

Tiff, who'd gone back to her room after eating too little for breakfast.

But Tiff wasn't in her room. She was in Lola's. Lying on the bed, crying softly.

Adora stood for a moment in the doorway. And then she kicked off her shoes and stretched out beside Tiff.

"You want to talk?"

Tiff bit her lip and vehemently shook her head.

"Okay, well, you know I'm here."

Tiff sniffed and nodded.

For a while they just lay there, side by side, as Tiffany cried. Adora thought of Lola, who seemed so close to them in this room. There were pictures on the walls: a few inexpensive prints of forest scenes and some photographs as well. Adora's gaze lingered on a family shot of Lola and Lemuel, with Tiff at about five, wearing a ruffled blue dress. And on another of a painfully young Lola holding a baby that must have been Jed. Behind Lola stood a dark-haired boy, her first husband and Jed's father, Billy Ryder. Lola had told Adora about Billy.

"It's the oldest story in the book. We were sixteen and crazy in love and the last thing we thought of was being careful. So a year later, we were married with a baby and Billy felt trapped. He enlisted when Jed was four. They shipped him off to Vietnam. And eighteen months later, they shipped him back to me. In a box."

Adora sighed, letting her gaze wander from the family photos to Lola's vanity table, which was made of some unidentifiable dark wood with a streaked triple mirror, a little padded stool and a brocade skirt. Arranged on top were all the things Lola used every day. A woman's things: foundation, eyeliners, blushers, face powder. Lipstick and mascara. An atomizer of Emeraude and body powder in the same scent. A cloth-covered jewel case. A silver-backed hand mirror that looked really old, with a brush and comb to match.

As Adora stared at the things on the table, Tiff suddenly spoke. "Oh, Dory, why?"

Adora's stomach clenched. And her secret guilt taunted her. I don't know why, Tiff, she thought. But if only I hadn't kept Jed at my place drinking champagne, then maybe...

Adora pushed the guilt away. It couldn't help Tiff. And Tiff was the one who mattered right now.

"I don't know, honey." Adora turned and opened her arms. "I just don't know."

With a little cry, Tiff scooted over and let herself be embraced, let Adora whisper to her the soft, meaningless words of comfort that people always offer when a loved one is lost.

"It's all right, you just cry. Just don't worry. Just let yourself go..."

Eventually Adora got up and went into the bathroom, returning with a cool, damp cloth. She laid it over Tiff's burning eyes. Then, when Tiff felt a little better, Adora urged her to rise and sit at the vanity table. Adora brushed Tiff's hair with the silver-backed brush. Then they sprayed some Emeraude into the air and sniffed at it. It smelled of Lola.

Tiff smiled just a little through her tears. "She really did come to me, in my dream."

Adora met Tiff's eyes in the vanity mirror.

"And she told me *never*," Tiff whispered fiercely, "*never* to forget that she loved me...."

Jed returned at a little before noon. When he walked into the kitchen, he was smiling.

Adora demanded, "What happened?"

"Wanda Spooner said she's real sorry about Ma."

"And?" Adora prompted.

"And she also said that since I'm Tiff's closest living relative, have a reliable source of income and appear willing and able to take the responsibility of raising her, everything should work out fine."

"And that's all?"

"No. She asked for a home visit. That's how they do it. They come here and look around and talk to us and see that everything is like it should be. And then Wanda makes her recommendation."

"That Tiff can be with you?"

"Yeah, that's how it looks."

That evening when Adora arrived home, she found a message from Cat on her answering machine. "Mom called. She told me Lola Pierce died. I'm so sorry. Call me."

Adora picked up the phone and dialed Cat's new number in Menlo Park. They talked for an hour. Adora told her sister all that had happened, and Cat listened and understood, the way she always did.

"Do you want me to drive up there?" Cat asked before she hung up. "Provide a little moral support?" For years, Adora had always turned to Cat when times got rough. But now Cat had a husband and a new life with him.

"No. I'm fine. But thanks for the offer."

"Anytime. You know that."

Adora was smiling when she said goodbye. It mattered a lot that she could count on Cat, that she had Cat to turn to if she really needed someone.

* * *

The next day Jed had to work and so did Adora. They agreed to meet at the house at four, so they'd be there waiting when Wanda arrived at four-thirty.

Tiff spent the day at the Shear Elegance with Adora, where the eleven-year-old made herself at home as she always had. She curled up on the white wicker settee in the waiting area, reading the magazines. She rearranged the product displays. And she answered the phone, when Adora was too busy with a customer to get there in time.

Most of the customers had heard about Lola. They expressed their condolences and were extra gentle with Tiff. Everyone spoke a little more quietly than usual, so the day had a kind of soft reverence to it. And early on, at a little after nine, Denita, who owned the donut shop next door, came in with a big, pink box full of donuts, most of them the cream-filled chocolate ones that Tiff loved.

"Tiff, come here," Denita commanded. "I've got your favorite kind. Lots of them." She wouldn't go back to her own shop until Tiff had eaten two of the gooey, sinful things.

Around noon, Jed called. He asked where Tiff was.

"I sent her out to get us some lunch."

"Can you talk?"

"Sure. Right now there's just me and Olga Hummerskild, and Olga's under the dryer reading the *Star*. Where are you?"

"Out at my place. Don Peebles called here. The autopsy's finished."

Adora's throat closed up when he said that, and the secret fear she'd been harboring leaped out at her with a vengeance.

He's going to say it now: if only we'd found her a few minutes earlier, if only I hadn't dragged him into my kitchen and insisted that he have a drink with me....

Jed was still talking, though not about the autopsy results. He was explaining that in a few minutes he was leaving for Reno. He had to make arrangements with a funeral home there. And he'd already called the Reverend Baker. The funeral would be held in the Red Dog City Methodist Church, Saturday at two.

"Yes," Adora said. "Okay." She tried to sound brisk and confident, but her poor heart seemed bent on betraying her. It pounded like thunder. Surely Jed could hear it on the other end of the line. Beating like crazy. Hurting her. With guilt.

"Adora?"

"Yes. Yes, I'm here."

"Adora." He sounded so gentle. Gentler than usual, even. "Peebles said she died of a 'sudden and acute cerebral hemorrhage.' A stroke, Adora. A big one. There was no way she could have made it. If it had happened in the emergency room of some major hospital, the chances still would have been slim to none."

"Slim to none?"

"It's not your fault. It happened. Nothin' you did, nothin' *anyone* mighta done could have changed it."

Adora clutched the phone tight and stared out the front window of the shop, through the white miniblinds, at Bridge Street. It was a beautiful day, the type of day California is famous for. "Are you sure?" It came out in a whisper.

"Positive."

Relief washed through her. Now she could just miss Lola, without having to secretly feel so tight and bound up inside.

"You okay?" Jed asked.

"Oh, yes. I'm okay."

He chuckled low. "Yeah. You do sound better."

"I was...feeling guilty."

"I know."

How could he have known that?

He answered her question, though she hadn't asked it out loud. "Adora, you're like lookin' through a glass door."

But then what exactly did that mean?

He went on before she could ask him to explain. "And I was feeling the same thing."

"The same thing? Wait a minute. You mean, *you* were feeling guilty, too?"

"Uh-huh."

"But why?"

"I kept thinking, if only I'd brought Tiff back to town sooner, if I'd moved faster to figure out where Ma was, if I hadn't hung around at your place for those extra few minutes. If, if, if. You know?"

Oh, she did know. She knew exactly. "Yes, I do. I really do."

"But it turns out the *ifs* don't matter. Nothing would have mattered. Nothing. It was Ma's time. Understand?"

She nodded, vehemently, not thinking that he couldn't see her.

"Adora?"

"Hmm?"

"Do you understand?"

"Oh." She laughed, feeling silly. "I do. Yes. I understand."

"So I'll see you at the house at four."

She hung up, smiling. And she felt better the whole rest of the day.

When Tiff and Adora returned to the house after closing the Shear Elegance, they found Jed waiting for them on the porch. He wore nearly new jeans and an unwrinkled T-shirt that actually had sleeves. He'd neatly tied his hair back.

"Lookin' good, Ryder," Adora told him.

Wanda arrived right on time.

The visit seemed to go well. Wanda looked around the house and talked to Jed about how he planned to care for Tiff. Jed explained that he made enough money to run the household and said that he was staying at the house now and planned to stay there indefinitely.

"And you said Adora's volunteered to be here for Tiff while you're at work?" Wanda asked.

"Yeah. That's the plan."

Adora spoke up, adding that ever since Lola had started working for her, Tiff had considered the Shear Elegance her home away from home. "I don't see any reason why she can't just go on thinking of it that way. I've always loved having her around."

Wanda nodded. "Sounds good."

Jed walked Wanda outside and lingered on the porch with her for a few minutes before the social worker left.

Adora stayed inside with Tiff, thinking to herself that it had gone really well. But then Jed came back in and she looked in his eyes. She could see that something wasn't right.

For Tiff's sake, Adora pasted on a bright smile. "I think it went fine."

"Yeah." Jed put his arm around Tiff and gave her shoulder a squeeze. "It went just fine."

Later, after Tiff had finally gone to bed, Jed suggested, "Let's go outside."

Adora knew he wanted to be certain that Tiff didn't hear them. She followed him out to the porch and took a seat on the step. He hitched a leg up on the porch rail just across the steps from her.

"Okay, what happened with Wanda?"

He didn't mince words. "She told me that Charity's suing for custody of Tiff."

"Oh, no."

"Oh, yeah. Charity's hired a lawyer. And the lawyer contacted Child Protective Services just this afternoon. The lawyer's filed a petition to get Charity and Morton temporary custody—until they can make it permanent."

Adora thought of Tiff, so miserable without her mom. This could make it much worse. "So what will happen now?"

"Right now, nothing."

"Tiff stays with you?"

"Yeah. Wanda says she'll recommend that Tiff should have the life she's been used to, as much as possible. That means living here. Having you keep an eye on her. Just what we thought."

"Well, that's good, isn't it?"

"For the moment. But if Charity stirs up too much trouble, Wanda won't be the only one making the decision about Tiff's future."

"What do you mean?"

He let out a long breath of air. "I mean it looks like I'm gonna need a lawyer of my own."

Adora closed her eyes and leaned against the railing post, taking that in. When she opened them again, she found Jed watching her. He looked so grim. As if Charity had already won the right to take Tiff away.

She sat up a little straighter. "Wait a minute. So Charity hired a lawyer. People hire lawyers all the time. That doesn't mean she'll get what she's after."

Jed shrugged. "According to Wanda, it'll come down to a judge deciding who can give Tiff a better life—me or Charity and Morton. I'm Tiff's closest relative. And I can prove that I can take care of her. But I'm single. With an *alternative life-style.*" His emphasis on the words made it clear that he'd gotten them from Wanda. "A judge could decide that Charity and Morton are a better bet to do right by an eleven-year-old girl than someone like me."

"They *could* win. That's what you're saying."

He stood from the railing and hooked his thumbs in his pockets. "Eventually. Yeah. They could win. Or they could make enough of a stink that Tiff would be shipped off to a foster home until a real decision is made."

Adora rose to her feet. "Oh, Jed. This is awful."

He ran a hand back over the crown of his head, smoothing the hair that he'd tied back so neatly in honor of Wanda's visit. "Yeah. Charity's married. She's home during the day. We gotta face it. Even if she's got a heart of stone, she looks good on paper. And that's what usually matters to a judge."

He let his arm drop and simply looked into her eyes.

Aching for him and for Tiff, she stared back at him.

And suddenly the idea was there. In the air between them.

Adora was the one who gave voice to it. "What if *you* were married? To a nice, *stable* woman?"

His eyes changed. They probed hers. And then he shook his head. "Come on. That's crazy."

"Just answer me."

He backed away. "Slow down."

She closed the distance he'd created. "What if you were?"

He said nothing.

A bird called out, one long, mournful trill of sound, somewhere in the night. "Jed. What if you were married? Answer me."

"Adora..."

"Just answer me."

He turned away, went to the end of the porch, where the glow of the porch light didn't quite reach. He looked out at the night.

"Jed..."

"All right, all right." He turned and faced her.

"Answer me. What if you were married? Would it make a difference?"

He nodded.

"A big difference?"

He nodded again. "Wanda even suggested it."

"That you get married?"

"Yeah." He let out a humorless chuckle. "She said, off the record, that if she were me, she'd find a solid citizen for a wife. And she'd find that wife yesterday."

Neither spoke for a while. The only sounds were the night birds and the crickets and, faintly, the light evening traffic on Bridge Street not far away.

This is insane, Adora thought. I can't marry wild Jed Ryder. Until forty-eight hours ago I hardly knew the man. And he's nothing like my dreams of who I'd marry....

But if she didn't marry him, Tiff would probably end up with Charity. And Adora really did believe that would be wrong for Tiff. So very wrong.

Jed seemed to read her indecision in her eyes. "Never mind. It's a bad idea. Forget it."

"No." She went to him, in the shadows. "It's not a bad idea." She lifted a hand and clasped his shoulder. It was like steel made flesh. As soon as she touched him, she wanted to snatch her hand away. She felt like a child on a dare, holding her palm over a flame. She would be burned—and yet nothing seemed so urgent as that she not let go. She willed her touch to communicate her sincerity. "Let's do it."

His light eyes bored right through her. "Are you messin' with my mind?"

"No. I mean it. Let's do it."

It seemed like forever before he whispered, "When?"

The enormity of it washed over her then. Her mind froze up. She gulped and let her hand fall to her side. "I guess, um…"

"*When?*"

She made herself consider the options. "We should get through the funeral."

"Fine. That's Saturday."

"And then maybe we could go to Reno. Sunday. Tiff could go with us. Okay?"

"Reno," he repeated, as if testing the idea for defects. "This Sunday." And then he shook his head. "No."

"What?"

"No. I don't want to go to Reno."

"I don't understand. Shouldn't we do this as fast as possible? So we can start showing we have the stable home life you were talking about?"

He reached out and touched her, as she had touched him moments before, clasping her shoulder. He looked hard into her eyes. "What we should do is make it clear that it's one hundred percent for real. We should do it like it's something we're proud of."

His other hand came up, to clasp her other shoulder. He held her gently. But her shirt had no sleeves. And his palms touched bare skin. It felt very...distracting.

She struggled to keep her mind on what he was telling her. "What do you mean?"

"I mean if we're gonna do it, then we do it right. A real wedding. With your family there—your sisters and your mother, too."

Adora's heart pounded harder; having her mother watch her marry Jed Ryder was not her idea of a good time.

He had such a strange look in his eyes. She wondered if he knew exactly how difficult that would be for her.

He was stroking her now, with those big, rough hands. Gently, so gently. Up and down her arms. "It can be small," he was saying. "Just the family and a few friends. But it should be here in town. We could put it together in a week, if we really worked at it. You could wear a white dress and I could rent a tux and Tiff could be the flower girl."

Adora's dazed mind focused on the inconsequential, probably to avoid the enormity of what he suggested. "Tiff's too old to be a flower girl. She'd be a bridesmaid."

"Whatever."

"And you told me you never wear straight clothes."

"So?"

"A tux is straight clothes."

"For my damn wedding, I'll make an exception. You're right when you say it should be soon. But I want it to be for real."

She tried once more to get him to see it her way. "Going to Reno's for real."

His hands stopped their stroking. They clasped her shoulders again, uncompromising, leaving no room for argument. "You stand up beside me. In front of the whole town. Or it's no go."

"Wouldn't people talk, about us having a real wedding so soon after losing Lola?"

"Do you really think I give a good damn if people talk?"

She stared at him. "I guess not."

"So decide. Will you stand up with me or not?"

Adora went on staring at him. He seemed so large right then. Larger than ever. Filling up her whole world with his strength and his heat, his contrary gentleness and his...unreadable outlaw nature. And it had all happened so fast.

Only two days ago her world had been empty. She'd been sitting in her pretty little kitchen, drinking good champagne. And then he had knocked.

And she'd answered. And nothing since then had been the same.

She felt, in some deep and complete way, that she knew him as she'd never known another human soul. And that he knew her.

Which was crazy. She didn't know him at all. He was wild Jed Ryder, and he was nothing like the guy she'd always dreamed she might marry.

But what good had her dreams ever done her? She was thirty-five years old. Mr. Wonderful in his Brooks Brothers suit would never come along—or if he did, he'd be like Farley. Using her and moving on.

She'd learned in the past forty-eight hours that she liked this man. And she respected him. She *admired* him. He was so good to Tiff. And he'd done so much for Lola.

And she even believed that she could live with him. She'd been practically living at his house the past two days, and if he had any really disgusting habits, she hadn't seem them yet. He helped with the dishes, and he picked up after himself. He was even willing to prepare meals, though Adora hadn't let him cook once yet; she'd taken over the kitchen because she'd always loved fixing food for people.

Tiff needed this, desperately. And the three of them would be a family. And above all, Adora prized family.

It wasn't perfect. But it could have been a lot worse.

"Make a decision."

"I...um..."

"Adora. Say you'll do it. Say you'll marry me in front of the whole town."

But she only stared at him, thinking of her mother, thinking of what people were going to say. Thinking of the way they'd whisper behind their hands as she walked up the aisle.

Jed swore, low and crudely. "You won't do it, right?"

"I, well..."

"You don't have the guts."

"I—"

And then, with no warning at all, he yanked her up against his rock-hard chest. He looked down at her, burning her with those light eyes.

She let out a small sound of bewilderment, of confusion.

His expression gentled. "Your eyes are green," he whispered, as if it were some kind of secret. "I like your eyes. They're honest eyes. Everything you feel shows in them."

"Jed—"

"Shh. Don't talk."

"But—"

And then, before she could get out one more word, his mouth came down on top of hers.

It was hot. His mouth was hot. And soft. And his mustache was silky against her upper lip. She gave a little cry.

He took advantage of that cry to deepen the kiss.

But gently. A gentle invasion. His tongue questioned. And teased. And knew exactly what to do.

Her hands came up to press against his chest. And then, within seconds, they weren't pressing anymore. They were holding on. And his arms were tight around her, holding her to him, while his hands were rubbing, massaging, feathering caresses down the small of her back, over the round curves of her hips.

Adora sighed, a deep, purring sigh. He made an answering masculine sound against her parted lips.

It occurred to her, vaguely, that even though they were in the shadows at the end of the porch, anyone walking by on the street would know exactly what they were doing.

She should pull away.

But she didn't pull away.

How could she pull away from this? This was much more than a kiss. This was...a whole new way of experiencing the world. Those feelings she'd denied the other day on Trout Creek Trail had been real after all.

Oh, she hadn't known, she hadn't realized, she'd never even *imagined!*

She could get used to this. She could. Oh, yes, she could!

Her hands were hungry, to touch and to know. She slid them up, over the hard warmth of his chest and wrapped them around his neck. Her fingers tangled in his hair, at his nape, above where he'd tied it back with the strip of leather. His hair felt silky, warm, alive to her touch. She wanted to pull off the leather strip, to bring a fistful of the black silk to her mouth, to breathe in the scent of it, to run the strands across her lips.

But then, as suddenly as he had pulled her close, he lifted his head. He looked down at her. She blinked up at him, dazed, lazy, deliciously weak with this new thing called desire.

"Say yes. Say you'll marry me here, in Red Dog City, at the Methodist Church, in front of the whole town."

She stared into those eyes that were like twin pieces of silver, hard as diamonds, and as bright.

"Say you'll do it," he whispered. "A for-real wedding. For Tiff's sake."

She clasped his shoulders, to steady herself. "I, um…"

"Say it."

She was nodding. And then she was answering, "All right. Yes. I'll do it. A week from Saturday. At the church. In front of the whole town."

He was smiling now, his hands stroking her, soothing her, rubbing down her back. "There's more."

"What?"

"We'll tell everyone it's for love."

"Love?"

He nodded.

"But that would be a lie. That would be—"

He silenced her with a finger against her lips. Down inside, she melted, just from that light touch. She wanted to open her mouth and suck that finger right inside.

His smile changed, grew knowing. As if he understood exactly what she wanted. He rubbed the side of that finger back and forth across her lips. She thought her mouth might just burst into flames.

"Listen," he said. "If it comes to a day in court with Charity, we'll look stronger together, if everyone thinks you married me for love." His finger trailed up, a long, light caress over the curve of her cheek. He smoothed her hair along the side of her face. Her body hummed. She felt like a cat—stroked, petted, purring somewhere deep down inside.

"For love?" he asked. "Will you tell 'em all it's for love?"

The words seemed to take form all by themselves. "Yes. All right. We'll say it's for love."

Five

Because she wanted to get it over with, Adora called her mother that very night.

The moment Lottie heard the news, she fainted dead away on the other end of the line. Bob revived her. And then Lottie got back on the phone and begged Adora to tell her it wasn't true.

"But it is true, Mom. I'm marrying Jed Ryder a week from Saturday. And I really hope you and Bob can be here for the ceremony."

"You can't do this. You'll ruin your life. Think what you're doing, Adora. Please. Listen to me...." Lottie went on and on. She ordered and argued and begged.

Adora listened.

But she didn't change her mind.

"Why?" Lottie cried. "Why would you do such a thing?"

Adora remembered her promise to Jed. She crossed

her fingers. "Because I love him. And I can think of nothing more wonderful than spending the rest of my life at his side."

Lottie gasped, but at least she didn't faint again. Adora listened to more pleading and a fresh onslaught of arguments, including how tasteless it was for Jed to be marrying so soon after his mother's death.

"I think Lola would have been pleased," Adora told her mother. And then she said she really did have to go.

She called her sisters next. Phoebe and Deirdre were almost as appalled as Lottie had been. But they promised to attend the wedding.

Only Cat—dear, steady Cat—was calm and accepting.

"Jed Ryder. No kidding?"

"No kidding."

"I always thought he got a bum rap all those years ago."

"Of course he did. This is sudden, I know. But I've been helping him out, the way I said I would, the past couple of days. He's a wonderful man. And we just seemed to…click, you know?"

"Love comes fast sometimes."

Adora swallowed. "It sure does."

"Adora?"

"Yes?"

"You *do* love him?"

"Yes." She willed conviction into her voice. "Very much."

"It's Saturday, the twentieth?"

"Umm-hmm. Over at the church, I think. Though I have to call and find out if it's available for that day."

"Wherever it is, Dillon and I will be in town by that Friday. With bells on."

"I know things must be hectic for you right now." Cat and Dillon were just getting settled in their new Menlo Park house, which was near Stanford University. Cat would be going to school at Stanford, starting in just a few weeks. With Dillon's help, she would fulfill a lifelong dream of earning an engineering degree. "Are you sure you can manage it?"

"Of course we can manage it. It's your wedding. I'd never miss an event like that."

The next morning at breakfast they told Tiff. She put down the piece of toast she'd been nibbling on and her eyes filled with tears.

"Oh, sweetheart..." Adora rose from her chair and went to her. "We didn't want to make you cry."

Tiff reached up and wrapped her arms around Adora. "This time it's 'cause I'm happy." She hugged Adora harder. "I'm happy, that's all...." She reached out for Jed, too, who got up from his own chair so she could hug him as well.

The next two days were busy ones. Adora ran the shop, handling both Lola's clients and her own. She looked after Tiff. She helped Jed with the last-minute details of Lola's funeral—and began making arrangements for the wedding, which was little more than a week away. She and Jed visited the clinic for their blood tests. And they ran off a flyer inviting anyone and everyone to the wedding. Tiff carried copies all over town, handing them out and tacking them up on every available surface, from the bulletin board at the post office to the telephone poles all along the town's three major streets, Commercial, Bridge and Spring. As it turned out, the church was still available. So they would be married there as Jed had hoped.

Adora knew, of course, that the whole town was talking. Lizzie had looked like her eyes might pop out of her head when Adora told her the news.

"But *why?*" Lizzie had cried. "He's not your type at all."

So she told Lizzie what she'd told her mother and her sisters. "I love him." She was finding it easier and easier to say.

"Wow," Lizzie muttered. "Too, too weird." But then she smiled. "He is kind of sexy, though. All those muscles, those silvery eyes and that diamond earring." She shivered deliciously. "And he doesn't go in for tattoos like a lot of bikers. I don't know if I could deal with a guy with tattoos." She shivered again and then asked eagerly, "What's it like, you know, when he makes love to you?"

"Lizzie, you're practically drooling."

"Oh, I get it. You haven't done it yet, have you? Not all the way."

"Come on. You're thirty-four years old. Have some dignity."

"Oh, *you* come on. He's kissed you, at least, hasn't he?"

Adora granted her a distant smile.

Lizzie clapped her hands. "He has, he has. Oh, what was it like?"

Adora couldn't help it. Her smile stretched wider. "It was just fine."

When Adora told Bobby Tamberlaine of her coming marriage, all he wanted to know was, "You happy?"

"Yes," Adora answered. "Very."

And really, the more she got used to the idea, the happier she was. Tiff wouldn't have to go live with Charity. And Adora would be part of a family again.

"Well then, congratulations," Bobby said.

Adora thanked him. Then, getting into her role, she sighed. "I just feel so fortunate, to at last be marrying the man that I love."

She wondered if she'd laid it on a little thick when Bobby chuckled. "So is the man you love through with my chinos and shirt yet?"

She made a face at him and promised to bring back the clothes the next day, which she did.

The service for Lola took place at two in the afternoon on Saturday, the thirteenth. The small church was full. Adora sat up front with Tiff and Jed.

Both Charity and Morton attended, sitting across the aisle and one row back. And they weren't the only Laidlaws who'd come to pay their last respects to Lola.

Dawn was there, too. Adora could hardly believe her eyes when she saw her, sitting next to her father. It had been a long time since Dawn Laidlaw Paulsen DeLongpre had visited Red Dog City. Everyone said that she lived in Santa Barbara now, since her second divorce.

Adora found the woman hard to ignore. After all, Jed had loved her once. Or so all the old stories went. And her beauty took a person's breath away. Her features were flawless, her skin like cream. She had silvery blond hair that looked as if it had been cut by Jose Eber himself and thick dark lashes, surrounding huge blue eyes. She wore gray. A perfectly cut gray silk suit and an ivory blouse, an ensemble that seemed to whisper, very tastefully, of money. Stealing a fifth or sixth glance at her, Adora felt depressingly ordinary in her four-year-old black dress and her grandmother's pearls.

And Adora could have sworn that Dawn kept looking at Jed, though Jed remained facing stoically front the whole time. Rumor had it that Dawn had ended up with a lot of money from her two rich, successful husbands. But she'd never found real happiness. Could she still be carrying a torch for Jed, even with everything that had happened all those years ago? And what would a woman with all that money and style see in wild Jed Ryder, anyway? Surely she'd become accustomed to much more sophisticated men.

But then again, Jed did have his own very special appeal. So far, all he'd done was kiss Adora once. And she couldn't stop thinking about what it would be like when they were married and sleeping in the same bed every night. Jed had done a lot more than kiss Dawn Laidlaw—or so all the old rumors went. And maybe, even after all these years, Dawn couldn't forget what they had shared.

Adora wasn't jealous. How could she be? She liked Jed, she'd even accepted the crazy fact that he excited her sexually, which no other man had ever managed to do. But it wasn't love, no matter what they had agreed to tell everyone in town. Still, Adora couldn't help feeling grateful that Dawn no longer lived in Red Dog City, where Jed couldn't avoid running into her all the time.

In the pulpit, the Reverend Baker had started to speak. Adora felt Tiff's fingers hesitantly brush her arm. The needy touch reminded her that her job right now was to help Tiff get through this, not sit here and fret about Jed's long-ago love. She took Tiff's hand in hers.

After the funeral, they buried Lola next to Lemuel Pierce in the Red Dog City Cemetery. A small reception followed in the church's social hall. Adora breathed a sigh of relief when none of the Laidlaws showed up for that. She assumed she could stop worrying about them for a while.

She was wrong. At nine that night, just after she returned to her apartment from the Church Street house, she heard a knock on her kitchen door.

When she answered, she found Charity waiting on the landing.

"I wonder if you could spare me a few minutes." Charity held herself rigidly erect, but she spoke more gently than usual.

Suspicious, Adora frowned at her. "What for?"

"May I come in? Please?" There was actual entreaty in her voice.

"I don't think—"

"*Please.*"

Adora hesitated for a moment, undecided. And then, though she knew it was probably a mistake, she stepped back and let Charity into her kitchen.

"This way." Adora led the woman to the living room, where she gestured at the couch. "Have a seat."

Charity perched on the edge of the couch cushion. "I won't take up too much of your time."

Adora sat in a padded rocker that she'd found at a flea market and had reupholstered herself. "All right. What is it?"

Charity folded her hands tightly in her lap. "I have heard that you and Jedediah plan to marry. Is that true?"

Adora kept her spine straight and her chin up. "Yes, it is."

Charity leaned forward. Her blue eyes shone with what really looked like honest concern. "But why?

You're from a respectable family. Why in the world would you want to marry a man like him?"

Adora had her answer ready. "I love Jed. And he loves me. We want to spend our lives together."

Charity's concerned expression turned to one of frank distaste. "That's absurd. Don't imagine for a moment that I buy a ridiculous lie like that."

Adora kept her cool. "I don't care if you believe it or not." She stood. "And I think maybe it was a mistake that I let you in here."

Charity rushed on, clearly intent on making her point before Adora threw her out. "Have you given a thought to the people who love you? Think of your poor mother. I am sure Lottie's just *ill* over this."

Adora bit down on the inside of her lip and reminded herself not to say anything she would regret later. "My mother is fine, thank you. She and Bob will do their best to make it to the wedding."

Charity shuddered. "Jed Ryder is an *animal*."

"Look. I think you'd better go now."

Charity surged to her feet. "Now, you listen here." She shook a finger at Adora, dropping all pretense of calm self-control. "I know exactly what you're up to. And it's not going to work."

"I don't know what you're talking about. And I've asked you to leave."

"Oh yes, you do. You know very well what I'm talking about. Jed thinks that if he's married, he'll be able to keep custody of poor little Tiffany. And for some reason, you have decided to aid and abet him in his scheme."

"I'm not aiding and abetting him. I'm *marrying* him. And I want you to leave."

Charity didn't budge. "You will hear me out."

"No, I—"

"I know you want a husband. Everyone in town knows that. But you mustn't do this. You mustn't settle for something like this, for a life of degradation with a *creature* like Jed Ryder. He will never make you happy, you must see that. And the marriage won't help Tiffany. It will only make it worse for her, in the end."

Adora stared at Charity in horrified fascination. The scariest thing about the woman was her absolute certainty that she was in the right. Who could argue with such fanatic conviction? Adora knew she never should have tried.

"I have asked you several times to go."

Charity drew herself up taller. "I am. I'm going. I just want you to understand that I will do what's good for Tiffany. In the end, no matter how ugly or expensive the battle, I will have custody of her. Because it's the right thing, that she be raised in a decent home."

Adora waited three beats. "Is that all?"

"Yes. As long as you realize that this meaningless marriage will get you nowhere."

Adora made herself smile. "Meaningless? It's far from meaningless. Jed and I want to make a life together. We *love* each other. So we're getting married. That's all there is to it. Now, may I show you the door?"

"I can find it myself."

"Good. Then please do."

As soon as she heard the kitchen door slam, Adora dropped to the rocker again. She was shaking a little. And more determined than ever that Charity Laidlaw would never get her mean hands on Tiff.

The next morning, Adora took Tiff to church. And then Tiff and Jed spent the afternoon together while

Adora drove into Reno and went shopping for a wedding dress.

She came home late in the afternoon with the dress she'd always dreamed of laid across the back seat—not to mention just the right shoes, a few gorgeous underthings and a negligee that had made the salesclerk sigh.

After dropping off her purchases at the apartment, she headed over to the house on Church Street to get dinner started.

But Jed had other ideas. "Come on. You, me and Tiff are going out to dinner at the Spotted Owl."

Adora dropped the potato she was peeling into the sink and turned to give him a huge, grateful smile.

The Spotted Owl was Red Dog's City's nicest restaurant. It served steaks and seafood and had a sort of cozy, log-cabin ambience, with wagon wheel chandeliers and a big natural stone fireplace. Adora had always liked eating there. The food was good and the service friendly. And next door was the Spotted Owl Tavern, where she and Lizzie and Bobby used to go to while away a few hours on long winter nights when snow blanketed the ground and the town of Red Dog City closed in on itself.

Jed had reserved a table in a private corner. They'd ordered their food and had just started on their salads when Dawn DeLongpre came in with a man Adora had never seen before.

Dawn and her date took a table several feet behind Jed—and in full view of Adora. Thus, through the entire meal, Adora was forced to watch Dawn sneak glance after glance at Jed's broad, leather-clad back.

"Somethin' wrong with that steak?" Jed demanded when Adora found her appetite had fled.

"No. It's fine."

He looked at her sideways. The diamond stud in his ear caught the light, winking at her dangerously. "Then eat it."

She picked up her fork. "I am."

Adora ate the steak—and tried her best to ignore Dawn. But she found it hard to drum up any interest in dinner. She just couldn't stop wondering if the beautiful blonde had something up her silken sleeve.

And she couldn't figure Jed out. He seemed totally oblivious to the other woman. But was he really? The whole thing set Adora's nerves on edge, made her wonder about the plans she and Jed had made. Just today she'd gone out and done serious damage to her bank account, buying her white dress and all the trimmings. She'd booked the church—as well as the social hall for the reception after the ceremony. She'd actually hired a caterer to prepare the hors d'oeuvres. And Denita, the donut shop owner, had promised to bake a three-tiered cake.

Adora had to admit it; she was having a ball getting ready to marry this man she hardly knew. And she looked forward to the life they'd have together—every phase of it, from raising Tiff to sleeping in Jed's bed.

But how did Jed feel?

Could he be having second thoughts?

Maybe, given a little time to think it over, he'd realized he hated the idea of being tied down. Maybe he resented Adora; it was necessary to marry her for Tiff's sake, but he wished he didn't have to.

Maybe he still loved Dawn. Maybe seeing Dawn and comparing her with Adora, he'd known at last what a whopper of a mistake he was making.

By the time the endless meal was finally over, Adora had come to a decision. She and Jed had to talk.

And since the wedding was six days away, it had better be soon.

The moment Tiff said good-night, Adora went looking for Jed. He wasn't hard to find. She just followed the sound of rock and roll and found him in the garage, fiddling with his bike. A huge black boom box sat on the workbench along the far wall, pumping out the Rolling Stones.

As Mick Jagger grunted and groaned, Jed removed what looked like a spark plug, polished it with a rag and stuck it back where he'd got it. Then he looked up and saw Adora. Wiping his hands on the rag, he sauntered away from her, around the front end of Lola's little foreign car, to the workbench. When he reached the boom box, he punched a button. Mick Jagger stopped grunting.

"What's up?"

Adora had to order herself not to fidget, to stand there calmly and meet his eyes over the hood of Lola's car. "I thought we could, you know, talk?"

There was a deep concrete sink a few feet from Adora, on the other side of the washing machine and dryer. Jed strode around the front of the car, past Adora to the sink, where he scooped some kind of heavy-duty soap out of a tin and washed his hands. When he was done, he reached for the towel on the nail near the faucet.

"Talk about what?"

"Well, I..."

His full lips curved in a hint of a smile. "Come on, Adora. Get it on out there."

So she did. "Dawn DeLongpre. Or whatever she calls herself now."

Jed hooked the towel back on the nail. "What about her?"

"She was at the restaurant tonight."

"So?" He turned to face her.

"She kept...looking at you."

"Is that my problem?" He leaned against the sink.

"Well, no. But..." She didn't know how to go on. And he wasn't helping. Not one bit.

He came away from the sink. "Then what *is* the problem?"

She found it hard to meet his eyes, so she looked down. The toes of his big black boots came into her field of vision. He put a finger under her chin, and her whole body started doing that humming thing again, like it had the other night when he'd shown her what a kiss could do. She could smell that hand cleaner he'd just used, a minty-gritty smell. She found the smell arousing.

He guided her face up so she had to look at him. "Talk."

She forced her senses to settle down and focused on what mattered right then: the truth about Dawn and Jed. "You loved Dawn once."

He shrugged and dropped his hand. "Yeah."

It was ridiculous, but that bothered her. It bothered her way too much. Why was that? She'd already known it. Why should his saying it out loud matter?

"You were *crazy* in love with her." She sneered the words.

He shrugged again. "Yeah. I sure was."

"And what about now?"

He wandered over and sat sidesaddle on his bike.

Then he spent a few long seconds just looking at her. "What *about* now?"

She glared at him. "Do you still love her?"

He stared at her for more long, hard seconds before announcing flat-out, "Hell, no."

Adora's heart suddenly felt lighter. "Really?"

He let out a long breath. "Adora. Why don't you just tell me what's on your mind?"

"Well..."

"Spill it."

"Okay. I guess I just want to know everything."

"Everything?"

"Umm-hmm."

"About me and Dawn?"

"Yeah." She slanted him a hopeful glance. "Or at least all the best parts."

He grunted. "You don't ask much, do you?"

She tried to look appealing. "Please?"

"Hell."

Right behind her were the concrete steps that led to the kitchen. She turned around and blew on the bottom one, to clean it off a little. Then she sat, carefully wrapping her skirt around her legs so the hem wouldn't drag on the garage floor. "I'm all ears."

He was shaking his head. But he was smiling a little.

She felt better all the time.

"All right," he muttered.

She gathered her knees up close to her chest. Since she wore sandals, she was able to study her toes, which were painted the same pinky-bronze as her fingernails. It was a pretty good color for her, really. She shot him a grin. "I'm listening."

"I loved her."

She wrinkled her nose at him. "You said that."

"And she loved me." He stared into the middle distance, no doubt seeing the past. "Or, at least, she said she did. And Charity hated that. Her precious baby girl was too damn good for a guy like me."

Adora recalled her unpleasant confrontation with Charity the night before. "I think I hate that woman. I didn't tell you she paid me a visit last night."

"Charity did?" At her nod, his eyes narrowed. "And?"

She shrugged. "It was just more of the same."

"Next time don't give her a chance to get started."

"I won't. Now go on. About Dawn. You said that Charity thought you weren't good enough for her."

"Right." Jed collected his thoughts, then continued, "Charity told Dawn she couldn't go out with me. So we'd sneak out to be together. And sometimes I'd climb in her window at night."

"And one of those nights—"

"—Charity caught us. Naked. Together in Dawn's bed."

Adora pictured the scene and a groan escaped her.

Jed nodded. "Yeah. It was a real grim moment, all right."

Adora leaned toward him. "But did Dawn really accuse you of rape?"

He scrubbed a hand down over his mouth and beard. "Dawn was as scared of Charity as that poor fool Morton is. She wanted me enough that she'd sneak out to be with me when Charity wasn't looking, but she wouldn't stand up and tell her mama that she was my girl. So when Charity found us, it got ugly fast. Charity started screamin', calling me a rapist, saying I'd *brutalized* her child. I yelled right back at her. I told her that I loved Dawn and Dawn loved me, and this wasn't any rape, it was just love. Just love, that was all.''

His eyes looked so sorrowful. "God. Lookin' back, I was nothin' short of pathetic. So sure that Dawn was gonna back me up. Babbling away about how much she loved me.''

"What did Charity do?''

"She turned on Dawn. 'He raped you,' she said, 'you know he did. Tell me the truth. Tell me that animal has forced you to do this.'

"I looked at Dawn. I didn't have a doubt she'd stand by me. But she was shakin' all over. And I could see the fear in her eyes. 'Yes, Mama,' she said, real low and scared. 'Oh Mama, he raped me. He did.'

"I just stood there, by the side of the bed, wearin' nothin' but the sheet I'd pulled around myself when Charity had burst in the room. I couldn't move, my heart hurt so bad. So I didn't move. I just stood there in that sheet until the sheriff's deputy showed up and took me away. I didn't give a good damn what they did to me. I just wanted to die.''

He shifted around on the bike a little, closed his eyes for a moment, then let his head fall back. He opened his eyes and looked at the Sheetrock ceiling overhead. "But I lived." He lifted his head, looked at her. "And when they got around to the police interviews, Dawn broke down and admitted her mother had scared her into lying. So the charges were dropped. But the damage was done.''

Jed looked away again. He fiddled with the wires and levers on the handlebars of his bike. "Ma was a wreck over what had happened, and my poor stepfather didn't know what the hell to do.'' He glanced up, into Adora's eyes. "He wasn't a bad man, my stepfather. But he was no better at standing up to Charity than anyone else was. I could tell that it would be better for both of them, for their marriage, for their life together in this town, if I was gone."

He fisted his hand and tapped it twice on the gas tank. "And I *wanted* to go, anyway. Hell, my damn heart was broke. I really was crazy for Dawn. And she did me the worst kind of dirt a girl can do to a guy. All I wanted was out. Away from this town. So I left. I dropped out of school and left."

Adora ached for him. "I'm sorry, Jed."

His eyes seemed far away, still lost in the past somewhere. But then slowly, they focused on the present, on her. "It's over. Long over. Dawn Laidlaw is nothin' to me anymore."

"But, Jed..."

"What?"

"Well, it's just that she still seems pretty interested in you. Honestly, Jed. She couldn't keep her eyes off you in the restaurant tonight. And she was sneaking glances at you during the funeral, too."

Jed got up from his seat on the bike. "So? She can look all she wants. I'm tellin' the truth. She doesn't mean a damn thing to me anymore. It was years ago. We were kids. And in the end, she turned out to be one of those girls who wants something wild to crawl in her window at night. Until she gets caught. Then she screams rape."

Distressed by his tone, Adora rose to stand opposite him. "Jed. You sound so bitter."

He was looking off into nowhere again, his mouth set in a hard line. But then he looked at her and his face softened. "Hell. Maybe I am bitter. A little, anyway. Who knows what my life woulda been like if Dawn

Laidlaw had stood up for me, said she loved me and was proud to be with me, rather than cryin' rape when her mama caught me in her bed? Maybe I wouldn't have left town at seventeen. Maybe I woulda finished high school, at least.''

Adora closed the short distance between them, wishing with all her heart that she could think of words that would heal the old wounds for good and all. But no words came to her. So she reached out, laid her hand along his cheek, felt the softness of his beard, the warmth of his skin.

He raised his own hand and captured hers. "Hey. Don't feel sorry for me. I don't need it. I'm doin' okay now. I'm doin' just fine."

"I...um..." Warmth moved out from his touch, down her arm, through her body, all the way to the top of her head and the tips of her toes. It was so hard to think when he was touching her. She'd just never ever felt the way he made her feel.

"You should see your face." He was smiling, a strange smile.

"Jed?"

"Yeah?"

"Are you...do you...?"

"What?"

"Do you still feel all right, about marrying me?"

He brought her hand to his lips and brushed his mouth along the ridge of her knuckles. "Yeah. I feel just fine about it. But what about you?"

Her whole body quivered. "Me?"

"Yeah." He laid her hand against his cheek again, smoothing it open, so her palm lay over his beard, and her fingers touched his earlobe and the tiny gleaming jewel there. "How do *you* feel about marrying *me?*"

Her lip was quivering like the rest of her. She pursed it to make it be still. He let go of her hand, but she didn't pull away. She rubbed her middle finger on the smooth, hard diamond stud that glittered in his ear. "I, um, feel fine, too. I don't mind marrying you at all."

He chuckled then, a sound that sent warm shivers along her arms and down her legs. And then he reached out, slowly, as if he didn't want to spook her. She gasped when he cupped her bottom in both of his big hands.

He smiled. And he reeled her in, pulling her up and against him, so that her hips were pressed to his. She felt that part of him that his jeans showed off so well. It was hard.

"Oh, my," she whispered, as she braced both hands on his chest.

He chuckled again. "'Oh my,' what?"

"Oh my, I guess you like me. At least a little."

"I do, Adora. I do like you."

"Well." It came out breathy, urgent, needful. "I'm glad."

He pulled her closer. She stood high on tiptoe, holding on to his black leather vest for dear life. It felt so good, to be pressed against him like that. Her body seemed to answer his—softening, yearning, readying itself. Her heart beat a hungry rhythm in her ears.

He bent his head and rubbed his nose against hers, slowly and deliciously, back and forth. She remembered the old rhyme from gradeschool: "Let's rub noses like the Eskimoses." She'd always thought that rubbing noses was the silliest thing. But now she understood exactly what the Eskimos must see in it.

He nipped the bridge of her nose with his soft mouth. "You're not a virgin, are you?"

He was certainly blunt. But that was okay. They *were* getting married, after all. He had a right to be blunt with his wife. She tried to be blunt right back, though she stammered a little in the attempt. "N-no."

He feathered a line of kisses over her cheekbone and up to her temple. "So then, is it big a deal to you, whether we wait until we're married or not?"

Her mind felt slow. She couldn't think. "Whether we wait…?"

He pulled back. She gave a small moan. "Shh," he said. "I'm here." And his hands on her bottom cupped her higher, snugger against him. He looked into her eyes. "You gotta give me a yes or a no. Do you care whether we wait or not?"

"You—you're so confusing."

"Naw. It's real simple." He bent his head and started kissing her again, his mouth moving over her cheekbone, his beard tickling, arousing. He whispered right in her ear, "I'm hot for you. I like you and I'm hot for you. And I want to know if you're hot for me."

"I…um…" She had to slide her hands up, hook them on his shoulders. Her whole body was turning so warm and weak.

But then something else occurred to him. The delicious kisses stopped. He raised his head and pinned her with those pale eyes of his. "Don't ever betray me."

She collected her shattered wits, or tried to. "I wouldn't. Not ever. I swear."

"Good." She wore clip earrings, little pink hearts. Holding her gaze as he did it, he lifted a hand and took them off, one and then the other, all the while continuing to keep her snug against his arousal with his other hand. He stuck the earrings in a back pocket of his jeans. And then he bent his head to her again—and bit her ear, ever so lightly, scraping his teeth along the sensitive lobe.

His rough whisper came to her. "Now, we're back to my question. Are you hot for me, too?"

"Jed..."

"I want you, Adora. Can I have you now?"

"I..."

"Say no. Say no now, or..."

But no was the last word on her mind.

He waited, giving her a chance to say it. But she didn't say a thing.

So he slid one arm under her knees, put the other along her back and hoisted her high. "Let's go to my room."

She wrapped her arms around his neck and buried her head against his chest. "All right. Let's."

Six

When they got to his room, he lowered her to her feet right inside the door. He left her for just a moment to switch on the lamp by the bed. Then he returned to her.

Swiftly and efficiently he took off her flowered skirt, her little pink lace-edged T-shirt and her sandals. He removed her pink panties and her matching lacy bra. He threw everything on a chair in the corner, except the sandals, which he tossed under the chair.

And then, by the soft light of the bedside lamp, he looked at her.

And she let him look. It was just like being touched by him, to have him look. And being touched by him made her forget everything, made the old dreams of that guy in the Brooks Brothers suit fade to nothing, to *less* than nothing. It wiped them out as if they never had been. All at once, she was someone else. Some woman she hardly knew, who lived so luxuriously inside her body and fully understood the pleasure that body could give her. Who *wanted* that pleasure. Who gave herself to it, with no holding back.

And really, this new woman wasn't a bad woman to be.

Naughty, maybe. But not bad. Not bad at all.

He took off his vest. And he took off his T-shirt. His midnight hair fell over his shoulders, long and soft as her own. The silver cross gleamed at her. His chest was so powerful, the muscles sculpted and sharply defined like the muscles of his shoulders and his massive arms. Black hair grew in a wedge, wide over the top of his chest and narrowing to a line that trailed down his hard belly and disappeared beneath the waistband of his jeans. Below the waistband, the placket stretched taut over the ready evidence of his desire.

He approached her, stopping just at the point where her bare breasts brushed his chest. Her nipples, already tight and hard, seemed to peak even tighter, aching with the need to be touched.

He glanced down. She knew he saw, knew he registered how her body wanted him, just as she had taken note of how his body wanted her.

He raised his big hands. She thought he would cup her breasts. And she wanted that, with all that was in her to want.

But he didn't. He clasped her shoulders, and then he began rubbing her arms lightly, the way he had the night that they'd agreed to marry.

He spoke, his tone soft and low as always. "You been tellin' everyone you love me."

She closed her eyes. His hands felt so good. If only they would just slide around to the front of her.

"In a minute." She could hear the smile in his voice and knew that *he* knew what she longed for.

She made herself lift her lazy eyelids. And he *was* smiling.

"You want my hands on you." Briefly, with a single finger, he brushed her nipple. "Here."

She licked her dry lips.

He teased, "Don't you?"

She nodded, her nipple burning and tight with the need to be touched again. And again.

"Say it out loud."

"I...want you to touch me."

"And you *have* been tellin' people that you love me. Haven't you?"

"Well, yes. Because we agreed that we—"

He put his finger against her mouth to cut off her excuses. "Haven't you?"

She bit her lip and whispered, "Yes."

He smoothed her hair, petting her. "The word gets out. You know how it is. People talk. In a small town."

Her whole body felt liquid. A river...a hot, flowing river. "Jed?"

"Yeah?"

"Won't you please...touch me?"

He traced her jawline. "I'm touchin' you."

"Jed. Jed, please..."

"Easy." He stroked her cheek, her temples, her hair. "I will. You know I will. It's just so good. To look at you. You're a woman who knows how to want, Adora. And you're a woman who knows how to give. That's special. You know that?"

She closed her eyes again, because all of a sudden, she wanted to cry. Two tears leaked out from under her lids and slid down her cheeks. He whispered something, so low she couldn't make out the words. And then he bent forward and his mouth was there, kissing the tears off one cheek and then the other.

He pulled back again. "I just want to hear you say it to me."

She stared at him, bewildered. "What? Say what?"

"That you love me."

She closed her eyes again. "But I..."

His voice came to her, soft and accepting. "You *don't* love me. I know that."

She opened her eyes and looked at him. Then why would he ask such a thing? Why would he ask for a lie?

He went on, so patiently, "I just want to hear you say it, that's all. I want to pretend."

"But, um, I don't understand."

"You don't have to understand. Just say it."

She opened her mouth, but no words came out.

He explained, "It's only a love game, Adora. A game men and women play."

"But I don't...I mean, I haven't."

"Haven't what?"

"Played that game."

He lifted one black brow. "You never told a man you loved him?"

She had to look away. She had told Farley she loved him. And she had believed it was true. At the time. But now...

"Adora?"

She looked at Jed once more.

"Never?" The word was a taunt, but a tender one. "You never told *any* man you loved him?"

She stared up at him, aching, yearning. "All right. I have."

"And do you still love the guy, whoever he was?"

"No. I don't. I don't love him. I'm afraid that maybe…"

"Yeah?"

"Maybe I never did."

He let the confession hang on the air a moment. Then he smiled. "So say it to me. Say 'I love you' to me. You're gonna marry me, after all. Come Saturday. And you've told half the people in town that you love me. Why not say it to me? Can it hurt?"

She was silent.

He prodded, "Well, can it?"

She shook her head.

He waited.

"I…"

"Yeah?"

"I, um…"

"Say it slow, Adora. Say it sweet and slow."

"Oh, Jed."

He did touch her then. He put his right palm against her left breast. She moaned. He touched the other breast with his other hand. And then he cupped them both. "I just want to hear you say it. Won't you say it to me? Please?"

Her head fell back. His hands were magic hands. So big and gentle—rough and tender.

"I love you." There. It was out. And his hands were so good, so right, so wonderful, rubbing her breasts, rolling her nipples, making her shimmer down below….

"My name. Say my name."

She could say that. She *would* say that. She would say anything. Anything at all. "Jed…"

His left hand went on fondling her breast. And his right hand trailed down, caressing her belly, until it reached the brown curls at the apex of her thighs. "Say it all at once," he instructed. "Say, 'I love you, Jed.'"

She hitched in a sharp, hungry breath and shamelessly lifted her hips toward his touch. "I love you...Jed."

And his hand slid between her thighs, to her most secret place, which was wet and wanting—starving for him.

And something happened. Something that had never happened before. All he did was slide a finger between her thighs. All he did was touch her, barely a breath of a touch.

And she shattered. Deliciously, totally. She cried aloud, in shock and wonder, and he caught her before her legs gave out from sheer delight.

A few moments later she came back to herself. He had carried her to the bed and laid her down upon it. She watched him, feeling boneless, drifting, dazed and dreaming, as he swiftly stripped off the rest of his clothes, the silver-buckled belt and the worn jeans and the boots and the heavy socks. And when he stood tall beside the bed, she understood that it was her turn to do the looking now.

And she did. At everything she'd already seen and lower, to the frank proof of how he wanted her.

And when she saw it, she gasped.

And he smiled.

Because Lizzie had been wrong. He did have a tattoo. Low down on his belly, so that it was half-buried in the dark thatch of hair there, and half-hidden behind his manhood, which stood so stiff and proud. It was an emblem. In red and black. The Harley-Davidson bar and shield.

"Nothin' rides like a Harley," he said soft and low. And then he threw back his head and laughed out loud.

Adora found she was smiling. And then she was laughing, too.

He came down on the bed beside her, stretching out, pulling her close. "Yeah," he said, as he lowered his mouth to hers. "I think we'll do just fine together, you and me."

He kept her there all night. And they didn't sleep at all.

He had a big box of condoms, and when he pulled them from the drawer before he loved her for the first time, she looked at them warily.

He read her face like it was a book. "Okay, what is it?"

"I just...well, do you bring a lot of women here?"

He set the box on the beat-up nightstand, next to the lamp. "No woman's ever been in this bed with me before. I bought these at Langly Drug, the day after you said you'd marry me."

She sighed. "You did?"

He grinned and rolled close to her again. "You bet."

A shining swatch of black hair had fallen forward over his shoulder. She wanted to touch it, so she did, taking it and stroking her hand down it, loving the way it felt. When she looked up at his face again, she could see he wanted to kiss her—and more. Much, much more.

She gave him a teasing smile. "Jed?"

"Yeah?" His tone was gruff.

And she said what he liked to hear, just the way he like to hear it: slow and sweet. "I love you, Jed."

And he reached for her, rolling her beneath him. His

body branded itself along the length of hers, and there was nothing, nothing in the world, but the feel of his flesh against hers—and, soon enough, inside hers.

They moved together, hard and fast, slow and sweet. A thousand different rhythms and all of them so right. So perfect. He did brand her. He tattooed her. With the pleasure he brought that was like a gift she'd never even dreamed of receiving. She cried his name. She swore she loved him. Over and over and over again.

In the morning, just before dawn, she thought of Tiff. "I should go home, change my clothes and come back. Don't you think?"

He lay sprawled beside her, one arm across his eyes. "Think? Who can think? Who *wants* to think?"

She giggled. "You're so bad. You're as bad as me."

"We're a pair."

"Yeah." She sat up and then leaned over him and traced the patterns of hair across his chest and down. "And in five more days we'll be married."

He caught her hand. "And you'll be here. With me. Every night."

"I will. But now…"

"I know." He released her. "It wouldn't make such a good impression on Tiff, right?"

"Exactly."

So they got up and showered together in the small bath off his bedroom. Adora had no intention of doing anything but showering. However, she just couldn't resist a few kisses. And soon they were both ready and wanting all over again, right there in the narrow stall, with the water pouring over them.

So Jed reached through the curtain for the condom he'd left on the edge of the sink, just in case. And Adora boldly slid it down over him. Then he lifted her and held her, with her legs around his waist, bracing her against the shower tiles and driving her over the edge one more time.

When finally he let her slide to her feet, she just knew she was going to be sore for a month. She staggered out of the shower and dried off. And then she dragged herself into the other room to pull on her clothes.

She was tucking her shirt into her wrinkled skirt when he came up behind her. His arms slid around her. They felt so good, so right.

She leaned back into his heat and his strength. His hands brushed the undersides of her breasts. She moaned, her body instantly heavy and hungry for him all over again.

His lips touched the side of her neck. She moved her head, giving him better access. He chuckled against her skin. ''Adora. You are somethin'.''

All she could do was lean back and whisper his name.

His teeth delicately scraped the side of her throat. She shivered.

He nipped her earlobe, then teased in a murmur, ''I just didn't want you to forget your earrings.''

She looked down. He had his hand out and the twin pink hearts lay in his palm.

She scooped them up. ''Thank you very much.'' Though her body didn't want her to do it, she resolutely pulled away and clipped on the earrings. She smoothed her skirt and ran a hand over her still-wet hair. Then she turned to face him. ''Okay. I'm out of here.''

''Adora...''

His eyes were gleaming. She knew that look. Her body knew that look. In one night, he had taught her body well. That look melted her. Melted her down to a puddle of quivering desire.

"Jed. I have to go."

He was wearing his jeans and nothing else. His bare chest looked so wonderful, still dewed with little drops of water from the shower.

"Jed. Really. You have to let me go. Tiff will wake up soon. And it just isn't right—"

"Say it."

"Jed."

"Just one more time. And you can go. For now."

"I—"

"Slow, Adora. Slow and sweet."

"I...love...you...Jed."

He smiled. "Okay. Move."

With a little groan she turned from him, her legs all wobbly and her knees like jelly. She heard him chuckle as she went out the door.

At her apartment, she found a message on her machine from her mother. Lottie and Bob would be there for the wedding. They'd come by car, spending a night in Las Vegas on the way and arriving in town on Wednesday.

"You *will* put us up in your spare bedroom for a few days, won't you dear?" Lottie's recorded voice sounded just a little too sweet. "Because you know I want to be there, to help out wherever you need me. Call me back, please. As soon as you can."

Lottie and Bob were early risers, so Adora called right then.

"Where were you last night, honey?" Lottie politely inquired.

Adora smiled to herself as she evaded the question. "Oh, gee, Mom. Things are just so crazy around here lately. I totally forgot to check my messages until this morning. And I have to get over to make breakfast for Tiff in a few minutes. But I did want to call you and tell you that I'm really happy you and Bob are coming. And of course you can stay with me.''

"Well, then," Lottie said primly. "That will be fine.''

Adora said again how happy she was that they were coming, and then told her mother that she had to go.

At the house on Church Street, she made toast and poached eggs. Every time Jed looked at her across the table, she felt her skin turning pink and her breath catching in her throat.

"Are you guys all right?" Tiff asked suspiciously, looking from Jed to Adora and back again.

Jed grinned. "We're great."

Adora nodded. "Yeah. Just great."

Monday was usually a slow day at the Shear Elegance. But not that particular Monday. In the shuffle after Lola's death, a lot of clients had missed their regular appointments. And several of them had chosen to rebook that day. So Adora worked almost straight through until four.

Though she hadn't had a bit of sleep, everyone told her how good she looked. And she hummed and smiled, and more than one customer remarked knowingly that being engaged to Jed Ryder seemed to agree with her.

Adora said, "Thank you, I believe you're right," and went on humming.

She and Tiff were already back at the house getting dinner ready when Jed returned from work. Adora was standing at the sink when she heard the roar of his bike. She caught one quick glimpse of him as he rumbled up the driveway and into the garage. And then the loud rumbling stopped. Silence echoed.

Adora waited, her heart pounding heavy and hard beneath her breasts, her whole body warm and quivery and weak.

Then, out of the corner of her eye, she saw the side door open. And then she saw Jed. She looked down, at her hands and the faucet and the head of red leaf lettuce she was washing. She washed like crazy to the sound of his boots coming her way.

And then he was there, his hands sliding around her waist, pulling her back against him. She smelled him, road dust and leather and man. And she felt him. Everywhere. All around and all through her.

"Jed."

He guided the hair away from her neck with a lazy finger. "Hi." He kissed the word right onto her skin.

"Oh, you guys..."

It was Tiff, sounding affectionate, but also embarrassed. She stood in the doorway to the living room, where she'd gone to watch TV after she'd finished setting the table.

Jed laughed and backed away from Adora, who stuck the same leaf of lettuce under the faucet for about the fifth time.

After that, they tried to be more discreet around Tiff. She really did seem thrilled with the idea of their marrying, but that was no reason to flaunt the more intimate side of what they shared before her innocent eyes. They did their best to wait until she was in bed to touch each other.

And then they made up for lost time with a vengeance.

Adora spent that night and the next wrapped tightly in Jed's arms. She slept no more than an hour or two in total. And yet, in the mornings, after rushing home at first light to shower and change, she returned to cook breakfast with a big smile on her face. And then at nine she went to the Shear Elegance feeling as if she could shampoo, cut and blow-dry every citizen of Red Dog City and still have enough energy left over for a foil wrap and a perm or two.

And beyond working and cooking and keeping two houses, there were all the wedding details to handle. Adora took care of them with ease. She and Jed managed to squeeze in the time to drive over to Quincy to pick up the license. She planned the reception and ordered the flowers. And she still felt as if she had energy to spare.

Energy she needed for the marvelous nights, when Jed made love to her as if he couldn't get enough of her. And that wasn't all. When they weren't making love, he would talk to her, so easily and comfortably, as if they were best friends.

He talked to her about how he'd learned his trade...

"From a legend. Dan Wise was his name. But he went by the Wise Man. Everyone called him that. He owned a shop in Panorama City that machined custom motorcycle parts. He took me in and taught me everything I know. He's dead now. Bought it about six years ago. Lou Gehrig's disease. It came on fast and took him down within the year. Bikers came from all over the western states for his funeral. It was a sight, all that chrome shinin' in the sun. And all those engines, loud and proud."

She'd wanted to know why they called him the Midnight Rider.

He told her, "For my long black hair."

"That's all?"

He chuckled. "No, it's not all. Also for that old Allman Brothers song. I almost wore the record out, playin' it over and over on the jukebox at a certain bar not far from the Wise Man's shop. And because my last name's Ryder—with a *y*, that's true. But who the hell cares? Half the guys I hung out with never did learn how to spell, anyway.''

Shyly, she'd dared to ask about his tattoo, about how he got it. And he told her that he'd gone to the best tattoo artist around, a guy recommended by the Wise Man.

''Did the Wise Man have tattoos himself?''

''You bet. Lots of them.''

''When did you have it done?''

''Fourteen years ago. The day I turned eighteen.''

''Why?''

''Because I wanted to. Because a Harley is freedom and a Harley was all I had. And that is a fact.''

And that got him started on his favorite subject: the Harley-Davidson motorcycle. Jed had a lot to say about Harleys.

''There's just nothin' else on the road that's a Harley. Never has been, probably never will. Anytime you hear one comin', you know it, you know that rumble.

''Let's tell it like it is. A Harley won't give you comfort. And a Harley won't really even give you top speed. Hell, the maximum speed of an unmodified machine is barely a hundred miles an hour. That ain't even close to the speed some of those rice burners'll hit. But no guy who loves his Hog gives a good damn about comfort or top speed. He gets on his Fat Boy, and gets out on the road and he just loves that bone-jarrin', hard-mounted ride.

''Because a Harley is everything that's truly American. It's big and mean. It's in your face. It's loud and it's tough. It's freedom. And like I said, for some guys, freedom is the only thing they got."

He looked down at her then, where she lay snuggled close to his side. And he smiled.

And then he laughed, which made a pleasant rumbling sound against her ear. "But don't be fooled. A lot of guys you see toolin' down the highway in black jackets and chaps aren't livin' on the edge at all. Not anymore. Hell. Half of them are weekend riders, nine-to-fivers, a lot of them rich. You never know anymore. You just never know...."

He pulled her closer, and she went eagerly, levering herself up to lie on his chest, so their lips almost met.

"Kiss me," he said.

Adora didn't hesitate. She lowered her mouth to his.

The kiss was long and deep and sweet. Adora gloried in it.

Jed was not the man of her dreams. And what they shared wasn't true love.

But it was good. It was very, very good.

She got out of his bed the next morning absolutely certain that everything was going to work out just fine. She went to work at nine, as always—and just happened to be standing at the register counter looking out the window when Dawn DeLongpre entered the donut shop next door. For some strange reason the woman kept hanging around town. But Adora didn't let it bother her. Jed had said Dawn was nothing to him anymore. And Adora believed him. She went on feeling good about everything.

Until two that afternoon when her mother and Bob arrived.

Seven

They arrived when Adora was alone. Tiff had gone to a friend's house for the afternoon. And Adora's last customer, who'd booked a perm, had canceled at the last minute. Adora stood at the window, closing the front blinds, when she spotted Bob's Cadillac Deville turning into the driveway next to her building.

She experienced a vague tightening in her stomach at the sight of the car, an unpleasant feeling of apprehension. At the same time she told herself that she was thirty-five years old, certainly grown up enough that the thought of dealing with her mother face-to-face shouldn't frazzle her.

But it did. Oh, it did.

Adora locked the front door and turned out the lights. Then, after pausing for a deep breath and to promise herself for the umpteenth time that she would not let her mother get to her, she marched out the back way to greet them.

Her mother was just emerging when Adora reached the passenger side of the car.

"Adora! Oh, honey." She reached out her arms.

Adora allowed herself to be thoroughly embraced. And then Lottie pulled back and held her at arm's length. Adora looked into the green eyes so much like her own and thought what she always thought when she saw her mother these days: that she was seeing herself, in thirty-odd years.

In addition to inheriting her mother's eyes, Adora had the same heart-shaped face and wide mouth. People always said that her mother was pretty. *And you are just like her,* they would add.

Adora knew the remark was meant as a compliment. And she tried to take it that way. But actually, she found it unsettling to be told she resembled her mother. She loved her mother. But she certainly didn't want to be just like her. She wanted to be her own person, unique unto herself.

Lottie was peering critically at her. "You look tired. Worn out, as a matter of fact."

Adora resolutely kept smiling. "I'm fine, Mom. Really." For three days now, everyone who saw her had said how great she looked. But not Lottie. Oh, no. Lottie thought she looked *worn out.*

"So how's the bride-to-be?" It was Bob, peering at her from around the rear of the car. He'd already popped the trunk and started unloading their bags.

Adora gently pulled free of her mother's grip. She went to Bob and stood on tiptoe to kiss his ruddy cheek. "I'm great. Just great." Bob was a big, sandy-haired, blue-eyed sweetheart. Adora had liked him from the very first time she met him, when he started dating her mother. "Let me help you with those suitcases."

"Naw, I can handle it. Grab Lottie's little makeup case, if you will."

They trooped up the back stairs with Adora in the lead. Inside, Lottie exclaimed over the redecorating Adora had done since their last visit. She thought the kitchen was "Lovely. So light and airy." And the living room, "A delight."

Bob thought things looked great, too. "There you go," he said, "raising the value of my property some more." Bob actually owned the building and gave Adora a terrific deal on her lease. In exchange, she tried to keep the place in good shape for him.

She led them to the spare room. "Make yourselves comfortable. We'll have a nice dinner over at the house later, and you can get to know Jed and Tiff a little. But right now, you can just relax and—"

But Lottie was already pushing her husband toward the living room. "Bob sweetie, you go on in and turn on the TV. I want a few minutes with Adora." She pressed herself against her husband briefly and gave him a light peck on the mouth. He patted her on the shoulder and then headed for the living room.

Lottie turned to Adora, a determined glint in her eyes. "Now. I want to say a few things. And I think it's best if I get them over with right away."

Adora reminded herself that she was not going to become upset. "What is it, Mother?"

They were still standing in the hall. Lottie apparently didn't like that. "Come on in with me." She waved a hand toward the bedroom. "Where it's private."

Adora simply didn't feel up to dealing with a lecture from her mother right then. She would probably never feel up to it, as a matter of fact. But certainly not right then.

"Mom, I can't talk right now. I have several phone calls to make. Wedding details, you know? And then I have to get over to the house and get started on dinner."

"Adora." Lottie looked hurt. "There are things that must be said."

"Well, I understand that. But not now. I have too much to do now."

Lottie sighed. "All right. When, then?"

Never, Adora thought. "Tonight," she said with a sigh of her own. "After you've met Tiff and Jed and the evening is over."

"Tonight," her mother repeated, sealing a deal. "Tonight before bed."

"Yes," Adora conceded. "Tonight. Before bed."

That evening at the house on Church Street, Bob sat in the living room watching television while Tiff and Lottie kept Adora company in the kitchen. At five-fifteen, Jed roared into the garage, home from work.

"Oh, my!" Lottie exclaimed. "What is *that?*"

Tiff patted Lottie's hand as the roaring stopped. "It's only Jed, on his bike."

"I see." Lottie pasted on a bright smile for Tiff. She and the eleven-year-old had hit it off just fine. "It certainly is loud, isn't it?"

"It's a Harley," Tiff said, as if that explained everything—which, of course, it did. She added with pride, "A '92 Softail. Customized by Jed himself."

"I see," Lottie replied. It was painfully clear that she didn't.

Jed came in the door a moment later, wearing his usual: grimy battered jeans and lots of leather. His hair was plastered to his head from the helmet he only wore because the law made him do it, and wild around the ends where the helmet didn't reach. A layer of grease and dust covered his face. Clearly, it had been a hard, dirty day at work.

"Jed." Tiff went straight to him and wrapped her arms around his waist.

"Whoa, easy," he said, holding his hands out. "You'll get covered in grease."

"So what?" She gave him an extra squeeze and then backed away.

Lottie, in a chair at the table, watched Jed and his sister with a sort of vacant-eyed, bemused horror. Adora left the counter where she'd been snapping green beans and made the introductions.

"Mother, this is Jed. Jed, my mom, Lottie."

Jed turned to face Lottie just as Lottie stood. They regarded each other. Adora's heart sank as she looked at them. They resembled nothing so much as sworn enemies forced to declare a truce.

"Well," Lottie said, after what seemed like about a decade, "hello."

"Yeah. Hi." Jed went on looking into her disapproving eyes for another long moment, then he turned to Adora. "When's dinner?"

Adora's hands were dry, but she wiped them on her apron, anyway. "About half an hour."

"I'm gonna clean up." And he left.

Tiff smiled hesitantly at Lottie. "He's kinda shy. But you'll love him when you get to know him better."

"Yes." Lottie sounded like a robot. "I'm sure I will."

Dinner seemed pleasant enough on the surface. Bob was warm and accepting, as always. He shook Jed's hand firmly on being introduced. And he asked a lot of questions about the machine shop and the vintage airplanes for which Jed made custom parts. Jed answered him easily, explaining about the number of men who worked for him, off and on, depending upon the sizes of whatever jobs he had in the works.

And Tiff seemed chirpy and animated. Once or twice, when Lola's name came up, her dark eyes grew sad. But then, within minutes, she would perk up again. And she ate an extra helping of lemon chicken. A hearty appetite in a child was always a good sign, Adora thought.

Lottie chatted with Tiff and Adora and Bob. She was gracious and complimentary about the meal. But she never addressed a single question to Jed.

And Jed had nothing to say to her, either. They took great care to ignore each other. Adora thought that both Bob and Tiff must have noticed it, though nobody said a word. They all pretended that everything was fine, a pretense which Adora found wearing. She felt relief when dinner was through and the dishes cleared away and Lottie started making those "time to go back to the apartment" noises.

They all gathered at the door, saying good-night. And then she felt Jed's hand grasp hers. She melted inside a little, as she always did at his touch.

"You leavin', too?"

She looked at Bob and Lottie, who were already beyond the threshold, waiting for her on the porch. "Well, yes. I—"

He cut her off. "Stay a few minutes." His voice sounded gentle, coaxing as always. But his silver eyes commanded.

"Uh, well—"

"Stay," he said again. And his grip on her hand told her very clearly that he had no intention of letting her go.

"Adora, come on," Lottie said sharply.

Jed spoke to Bob. "You two go ahead. She'll be there. In a while."

Lottie looked slightly frantic. "Adora?"

"Um, look. You guys go on back to the apartment. I'll be there soon."

"But—"

Bob took Lottie's arm. "See you then." He guided Lottie around and led her down the steps.

Right then the phone rang.

"It's Mindy," Tiff sang out, already turning toward the sound. Mindy was the friend Tiff had played with that day. "I'll get it. In my room." Seconds later she disappeared down the small central hall.

Jed released Adora's hand, then reached out and pushed the door closed. "What the hell's going on?"

Adora backed away from him, toward the center of the room. "What do you mean?"

"I mean, your mom hates my guts. And you were leavin' with her, just walking out without a word to me."

Adora decided to try a little equivocation. "I wouldn't say she hates you. Exactly."

He made a sound of pure disgust. "Then what would you say? Exactly."

"Well..."

He grunted. "She hates my guts."

"Jed, Tiff is—"

"Busy on the phone in the other room. Don't worry

about Tiff. Stick to the subject. Are you gonna let your mama mess us up?''

"No. No, of course not.''

"She's gonna be talkin' to you. She's gonna be workin' on you. You know that, don't you?''

"I...''

"No lies, Adora.''

She sank to one of the flowered easy chairs. "All right. I know it.''

He came and stood over her, looking down. His eyes were so sad. "If she's gonna break you, I want to know now.''

Adora drew in a long breath. "She isn't going to break me. I promise you.''

He gave her one of those long, probing looks of his. She forced herself not to fidget, to meet his gaze levelly.

At last he muttered, "I guess you gotta go over there.''

"Yes. I think that would be best. They are my guests and I—''

He waved his hand, cutting off her excuses. And then he looked at her some more. The glory of the nights they'd spent together seemed to rise up and hang, shimmering, in the air between them.

"It's only a few nights, Jed,'' she heard herself murmuring huskily. "And then we'll be married. We'll sleep together every night, and nothing will keep us apart.''

He reached out, and his hand whispered along her cheek. "You let her have a go at you. And when she's done for the night, you make them comfortable. You settle them in. And then you come back to me.''

"But, Jed...''

"Come back.''

"Jed, it will only make trouble. I think it's better if we just—"

He shook his head. "I'm thirty-two. And you're thirty-five. We're grown-ups. Married or not, what we do at night alone is our own damn business."

"Yes, but—"

"Come back. I want to see your face. After she's through workin' on you for the night."

"Jed..."

"Come back."

She could not deny those eyes. "All right." She sighed. "I'll come back."

At her apartment, Adora found Bob already settled comfortably in front of the TV. He looked up and smiled just as Lottie appeared from the guest room.

"There you are." Lottie reached for Adora's hand and then pulled her straight to the guest bedroom. "Now, honey," Lottie pushed Adora down on the side of the bed and then perched next to her. "It's time for our talk." She put her arm around Adora. "I really won't feel right with myself unless I've been frank."

Adora cast a cold glance at the hand that was wrapped around her shoulder. "Fine, Mom. Be frank."

Lottie dropped her hand. "You've got that stubborn look you used to get when you were little."

"But I'm not little anymore, Mom."

"Of course you're not."

"So how about if you just say what you think you have to say?"

"Well, first I would like to know that you'll let me finish. That you won't interrupt until I'm done."

"All right, Mom. I won't interrupt."

"Wonderful." Lottie folded her slim, soft hands in

her lap and looked down at them, gathering her thoughts. Then she looked up at Adora.

"I know it's a difficult time for you," Lottie began. "I realize that you're a born homemaker with no home to make. That you want a husband desperately. I'm no scientist, but I do understand the concept of the biological clock. And I know yours must be ticking so loudly that it's keeping you up nights."

Lottie stared at her hands again. "And, honey, I know that you have felt deserted, by your family. With me and Bob all the way out in Arizona. And all three of your sisters married and moved away. I understand that. I truly do.

"But Dory, none of that is reason enough to marry a horrible biker person. Oh, honey. You must have heard the rumors about that man over the years. He is dangerous. And he toys with women. You know what happened to poor Dawn Laidlaw, what he did to her. The poor girl's life was ruined."

Adora couldn't keep silent in the face of that. "Mother, Jed did not ruin Dawn Laidlaw's life. If anything, she was the one who—"

"Are you going to let me finish? You said you would."

Adora rubbed the back of her neck, where the muscles had suddenly decided to tie themselves into knots. "Okay. Go on."

"Oh, sweetie. How can I put this? How can I say it so it doesn't sound hard and crude? There is just no other way. I'm just going to have to be horribly blunt."

Adora couldn't help asking grimly, "Blunt about what?"

Lottie squirmed a little, then she forced herself to sit still. She sucked in a huge breath to fortify herself.

And then she announced, "Adora, I can see by the dazed, dreamy expression on your face when you look at him, that Jed Ryder has been toying with *you*. Honey," Lottie pitched her voice low, in accordance with the extreme sensitivity of the subject matter, "you're letting your sex urges blind you to the truth."

"Mother—"

"No, no. I'm not finished. The truth is that a little exciting sex will not make a marriage work. You'll never in a hundred years be happy with a man like that. Not in the long run. You know the kind of man you've always wanted. You've told me a hundred times. You want a *successful* man, or at least a man on the way up. A go-getter, a professional. That's what you've always said. And yet, here you are, with this *outlaw*. It's insane. It simply won't last. So why ask for heartbreak?"

Adora longed to say it right out: I'm marrying Jed for Tiff's sake. But she couldn't do that. She'd promised Jed she'd tell everyone she loved him. And she would keep that vow. It could make a difference, if they ever ended up in court.

"Honey, have you heard me at all?"

Adora looked away. Her mother was wrong about Jed, terribly wrong. Jed was a good man. But Lottie was right about the rest. She was crazy for Jed physically. And Jed was not the man she'd dreamed of marrying.

"Honey?"

Adora stood. "Have you said it all, Mom?"

"Well, I—"

She put up a hand. "Are you finished?"

Lottie straightened her shoulders. "Yes. Yes, I am."

"Okay, then. I've heard you. Every word. And you are wrong."

"Dory—"

"It's my turn now."

Lottie looked pained, but resigned. "Yes. All right. Go ahead."

"Jed Ryder is a wonderful man. I won't go into details, since I'm sure you won't believe me, anyway. But I know he's wonderful. And if you love me, you will keep your bad opinions of him to yourself from now on. You might even go so far as to give him a chance to show you the kind of person he is. But that's up to you. You have your life, Mother. And I am going to have mine. I love Jed Ryder."

She must have sounded convincing, because Lottie muttered sadly, "Oh, this is bad. Very bad."

"Well, you'd better put a good face on it. Because I am marrying Jed on Saturday. Period."

After that, there wasn't much more to say. Her mother tried to muster up a few new arguments, but Adora only stared at her, waiting for her to let it be.

Finally Lottie asked for a hug, which Adora gave her. Then they joined Bob in the other room, where he was watching a war movie on cable.

Adora resigned herself to entertaining them for an hour or two. Then, when they went to bed, she would let herself out quietly and go to Jed.

"How about some popcorn?" she asked.

"Why, that would be lovely," her mother sweetly replied.

So Adora made popcorn and served soft drinks.

And when the war movie was over, Lottie decided to watch *Casablanca*, which was on right after it.

It was getting a little late. Adora knew Jed would be waiting. And wondering. She tried to sound teasing when she remarked, "I thought you two always went to bed by ten."

Lottie gave her another in a long series of angelic smiles. "Tonight, we're a little keyed up."

Say it, Adora's braver self urged. *Tell her you're going back over to Jed's.* But somehow, she just couldn't do it.

She heard herself suggest, "Gee, I am really pretty tired."

"Well, then go on to bed, honey. Don't let us keep you up."

It was nearing midnight when Bob and Lottie finally called it a night.

Adora lay, fully dressed, on her own bed, listening to the sounds of water running in the bathroom, waiting for the door to the guest room to close and silence to follow. At last it did.

Feeling like a naughty teenager and thoroughly despising herself for tiptoeing around in her own apartment, Adora rose from the bed and reached for her sandals, which she wouldn't put on until she was safely down the back steps. She was at the door, slowly turning the door handle, when something pinged on the window that looked out on the street.

She swiftly padded over there and looked down.

It was Jed, standing on the sidewalk, the streetlight a few feet away making his hair shine like a crow's wing. He stared up, waiting.

She turned on the lamp so that he could see her. And then she gestured that he should meet her in back.

Less than a minute later, she was closing and locking her back door. Lightly she ran down the stairs. Jed materialized from the shadows as she was leaning against the building, slipping her sandals on her feet.

He whispered, "I thought you weren't coming."

In the dim light, she couldn't read his face at all. "I was just—"

"—waiting for them to go to bed." It sounded like an accusation.

She slipped the strap of the second sandal over her heel and stood away from the wall. "I just would like to avoid trouble, Jed. I really would."

"You're sneakin' out. Right? Like some kid."

"Jed—"

He made a low sound in his throat. "Hell. Never mind. I'm helpin' you. Throwing rocks at your window, instead of marching up to your door and knocking, like any man with pride would do."

She put her hand on his muscle-knotted forearm. "Come on. Let's just—"

Lightning-fast, he grabbed her and hauled her up tight against him. He whispered, "What did she say to you?"

She braced her hands on his chest and whispered in return, "Tiff's alone at the house. We should get over there."

"Tiff's sound asleep. Answer me."

She was not going to tell him what her mother thought of him. He already knew anyway. "She said she thought I was making a mistake. That you weren't the right man for me. That our marriage wouldn't last."

"So you told her it was for Tiff, right?"

"No, I did not."

"What did you tell her?"

"That I love you. And that she'd better get used to it, because nothing would stop me from marrying you on Saturday."

His hard grip gentled. He began caressing the curve at the small of her back. "You did?" Even through the dark, his eyes were gleaming. His white teeth flashed with his smile.

"Yes. Now can we please go to the house?"

"You're somethin', Adora."

"I mean it, Jed. Let's go."

"One kiss first."

"Jed—"

He cut off her arguments with his wonderful mouth. It closed over hers and his tongue came inside and she melted all over.

When he lifted his head, she stared up at him, dazed and weak and thoroughly aroused, as she always seemed to be with him.

He stepped back and took her hand. "Come on. Let's go." He took off at a run.

Adora ran to keep up with him, stumbling, giggling a little, out to the street and down to the corner and straight to the house and the room over the garage.

Once they reached that room, he started kissing her again. He kissed her right up against the closed door. And then, while he was kissing her, he unbuttoned his fly and pulled a condom from his back pocket. He slid it on.

And then he raised her skirt and pulled down her panties and tossed them swiftly out of the way. And then his hands were on her, moving down the backs of her thighs, stroking, then lifting. She settled onto him, moaning joyfully, her back braced against the door, wrapping her legs tight around his hard waist, murmuring the words of love that he liked to hear.

The completion claimed them both at the same time. Adora felt him, pulsing, and then she was pulsing, too, and the whole world was shimmering, breaking gloriously apart.

Moments later they lay together on the bed. And Jed

was kissing her lazily, unbuttoning her buttons and sliding all her clothes away. She kissed him back, helping him off with his clothes as he worked on hers.

At last they were both naked. The night caressed them. And the slow, long time of touching and caressing began all over again. Jed kissed her everywhere, his mouth trailing down to the secret heart of her. She held his head, stroked the long black hair, as he kissed her there, deep and sweet and tender and good, until she was pulsing with fulfillment all over again.

Adora opened her eyes to daylight. Jed was wrapped all around her, one arm under her head, the other at her waist. Long silky strands of black hair tangled with her own brown curls, and one of his legs lay across her thigh. She turned her head to look at the clock. It was well past seven.

"Oh, no."

"Huh, what?" Jed groaned and stirred.

Adora untangled her limbs from his and jumped from the bed. She ran around the room, grabbing up her clothes and then, when she had most of them, yanking them on. As she frantically buttoned up her dress, she heard a low chuckle from the bed she'd just leaped out of.

She threw her sandal toward the sound, not intending to hit him, just to make him stop that irritating chuckling. He reached up as it sailed toward the wall, catching it neatly.

Once he caught it, he looked at it, faking surprise to see it there in his hand. And then he waved the darn thing at her. "You're gonna get caught. You are b-a-d. And now your mama will know."

She slid on the other sandal. "Keep it to yourself,

Ryder. I've gotta go." She limped over to the bed and held out her hand. "Give that to me."

He wiggled his black brows at her and flicked the sheet away from his belly, so she could see his Harley-Davidson tattoo—and everything else, as well. "Oh, baby. You know I love to give it to you."

She wanted to laugh. And to jump on him and kiss him. And she had to get going. Now.

She grabbed for the shoe; he held it away.

"Jed!"

"Say it."

"Jed Ryder."

"Come on. Just once. Slow and sweet, like only you know how."

So she did. "I love you, Jed."

He held out the shoe toward her.

And when she reached for it, he grabbed her.

"Jed! Oh, you…"

And they went rolling across the bed, laughing and kissing. And then they weren't laughing. And the kisses got longer.

"Jed. I really have to—"

"Okay, okay." He claimed one more kiss and then at last he let her go.

She sat on the edge of the bed and slid on the other sandal. "I'll be back, in an hour or so."

"I know."

She bent close to him for one last brushing kiss. And then she jumped to her feet and ran down the stairs and out through the side door of the garage.

Minutes later she let herself in the kitchen door—and found her mother, sitting at the table in her quilted aqua blue bathrobe, waiting for her.

Eight

There was nothing to do but show a little dignity. "Good morning, Mom."

Lottie regarded her daughter in outraged disapproval. "I do not believe this."

"Oh, really? Where's Bob?"

"He's sleeping in. And I'm relieved about that, at least. I'd hate for him to see you now. Your hair is a tangled mess. And your dress... Words fail me. You know very well what you look like, don't you?"

Adora decided she could use a little caffeine. She went to the pot that Lottie had already made and poured herself a cup. Then she took a chair opposite her mother.

Lottie was fuming. "You crept out and spent the night with him, didn't you?"

Adora took a sip of the coffee. Its warmth was welcome. "Yes. I did." She set her cup down, wondering why she hadn't just told her mother the truth last night, borne her heated protests then, and spared them both this absurd confrontation this morning.

"What about poor little Tiffany?" Lottie demanded.

"How will she ever know? Unless you tell her."

Her mother sniffed, thoroughly affronted. "Why, I would never do such a thing."

"Then there's no need to worry about her, now is there?" Adora drank more coffee.

Lottie released a heavy sigh. "Oh, Adora..."

Adora set down her cup again, more firmly than the first time. "Mom. Give it up. I told you last night, this is my life and you're going to have to let me live it."

"But I just can't bear to see you—"

Adora interrupted, "Learn to live with it. Or don't. That's your business. But I have a lot to do in the next two days. Are you here to help me or just to make things tougher?"

Her mother blinked. "Why, I—"

"Look, Mom. You're going to have to choose whether to work with me here. Or to just go on home."

A muscle twitched under Lottie's left eye. "What? Go home? *Now,* you mean? B-before the wedding?"

"Yes, that's exactly what I mean."

"But I don't—"

"Yes, you do. You understand perfectly. I love you, Mom. And that isn't going to change. But I don't want you here if you're going to do nothing but make predictions of doom, lecture me about how I spend my nights—and be rude to Jed every chance you get."

Lottie shook her head. "Well. I don't...I just had no idea..." She stared at her daughter. "You would send me away?"

Adora answered with honest regret. "Yes, if I have to."

Lottie pulled her robe closer. "I want to help. I do."

"Good."

"And I love you." Lottie rested an arm on the table and leaned toward Adora. "You know I do."

"I know."

Lottie looked down, into her coffee cup. "Bob told me to stay out of it."

Adora reached across the table and put her hand over her mother's. "You should listen to Bob."

After breakfast, Lottie and Bob took Tiff to Reno in search of a dress for her to wear to the wedding. While they were there, they ran some errands, picking up a long list of items Adora had yet to get around to buying. When they returned, Lottie got right to work, going over the music list with the church pianist and checking to be sure that all the tables and chairs and tablecloths and dinnerware would be at the social hall as planned on Saturday morning. She paid a visit to Susie Keeling, who catered parties in her spare time and was providing some simple hors d'oeuvres for the reception.

And that night, when they all sat down to dinner at the Church Street house, Lottie was painstakingly polite to Jed. Like the night before, Adora went back to the apartment with Bob and Lottie to see them settled in. Jed didn't put any pressure on her to return to him.

But she returned, anyway, at a little past ten, after saying good-night to her guests.

At the house, she found the garage door open and the garage light on. Jed had his head under the hood of Lola's car. From the boom box, Bob Seger's rough voice rolled out, a song about long nights on the road.

When Jed realized he had company, he closed the hood and turned off the boom box, then he pulled down the garage door.

They looked at each other. Adora was thinking of Lola. "Your mom had that car for years and years. She gave it a name, even."

He grunted. "I remember."

They said it together, "Sparky," and then they both laughed.

Adora said, "I wish she was going to be here on Saturday."

He looked at her sideways. "If she could be here, we wouldn't be gettin' married, remember?"

She felt foolish. "Right. Of course. But you know what I mean."

"Yeah. Sure. I know what you mean."

There was a silence. Adora usually didn't mind silences with Jed. But this one had an edge to it, a feeling of things unsaid.

She coughed. "Something wrong with it?"

"What?"

"The car."

"Oh." He shrugged. "I was just givin' it a once-over. It looks like the carburetor's shot. And it leaks oil. Still, it's a decent little car. Maybe I'll fix it up. Sell it."

"Maybe Tiff will want it someday."

He shrugged. "By the time Tiff needs a car, we can get her something a little nicer."

She waited as he wandered over to the sink and cleaned his hands. Then he came to her and touched the side of her face. She smelled that hand cleaner and smiled, thinking of their first night. Was it possible that it had been less than a week ago?

"What's that smile mean?"

She traced one of the zippers on his vest. "Oh, just thinking."

"About what?"

She lightly touched the silver cross. "You."

He slipped his hand around her waist. "That's good."

"Yeah. It is." She looked up from the cross and into his eyes. "Tiff in bed?"

"Uh-huh."

She was wearing enamel earrings shaped like daisies. He slid them off, one at a time, and made them disappear into a pocket of his vest.

Then, with the hand that wasn't holding her close, he began stroking her hair. "What did you do to your mom?"

"We had a talk this morning."

One side of his mouth curled upward. "You drew the line, didn't you?"

"I did."

He kissed the tip of her nose. "I like a woman who knows how to draw the line."

She stood on tiptoe and rubbed her cheek against his beard, shivering pleasantly at the gentle friction. "Why, thank you."

"Welcome."

She turned her head a little, and their lips met, sweetly, lightly. "Umm..."

He caught her lower lip between his teeth, and then released it. "Adora?"

"Hmm?"

"I heard somethin' on the job today. From Spike, one of my men."

She pulled back.

Jed frowned. "What? You know Spike?"

Reluctantly she admitted, "Yes. I know him."

"How?"

She made a face. "Last winter, he tried to pick me up, over at the Spotted Owl Tavern."

Jed's frown deepened. "Spike put the make on you?"

She nodded. "And I turned him down. He didn't like that. He got pushy. And Cat was there, in a real bad mood. It was just before she and Dillon got together. She was totally gone on him already. But she didn't want to be, so she was keeping away from him. Anyway, Spike wouldn't leave me alone. And Cat was in such a weird mood. She decided, for some crazy reason, to defend my honor."

Jed whistled. "Against *Spike?* Spike's two hundred twenty pounds of solid muscle. Your sister's no wimp. But she can't weigh more than one-twenty soaking wet."

"Tell me about it."

"What happened?"

"It worked out. Dillon appeared out of nowhere—and Spike and his buddy, Dooley...you know Dooley, don't you?"

"Yeah. He's on my payroll, too. Spike and Dooley what?"

"They turned out to be big fans of daredevil Dillon's. They'd seen every jump he ever did, they said. So they forgot all about trying to get a date out of me and decided not to beat up Cat after all. Dillon ordered a round on the house, and they went over to the bar with him, and he told them a bunch of stories about riding motorcycles through the roofs of barns and stuff like that."

"Has he bothered you since?"

"Spike?" Once or twice she had caught the biker looking at her on the street. But that was hardly being bothered. "No, he hasn't. Not at all. Now, what did he say to you today?"

"If he bothers you, you let me know."

"I will, I promise. Now tell me what he said."

"He said the word is out, about the wedding. I just wanted to warn you, that's all."

"Warn me?"

"There could be bikers in town. A lot of them."

"Because you're getting married?"

"Yeah."

"Is that something bikers do, show up for weddings?"

He looked uncomfortable. "Depends on whose wedding, I guess."

"Then why yours?"

"Adora..."

"Come on. Tell me."

He made a gruff sound in his throat. "It's somethin' no other biker who ever knew me would expect, that's all."

"It is?"

"Yeah."

"Why?"

"I always swore to keep my freedom. I swore that no woman would ever tie me down." He was grinning again. "I guess a lot of guys just want to see the woman who made a liar out of the Midnight Rider."

"What will they *do*?"

"Nothin' much."

Adora looked doubtful.

Jed reassured her. "I swear. They'll ride around town

some, and they'll hang out at the Spotted Owl. And they'll give us an escort out of town after the wedding.''

"An escort?''

"Yeah. A motorcycle escort. A big one. They'll ride out behind us in double rows.''

"My mother will go nuts.''

"Yeah, she probably will.'' He seemed to find the idea enjoyable.

"Have some sympathy for my poor mother.''

He snorted. "Yeah. Right. Like she's got sympathy for me.''

She faked a stern expression. "You don't deserve sympathy, Jed Ryder. You are b-a-d.''

He grabbed her then, scooping her up and hoisting her high against his chest. "Let's go upstairs. I'll show you just *how* bad.''

She nuzzled the side of his neck. "I know you will. I'm counting on it.''

"I wouldn't want to let you down.''

"Oh, you won't. You never have yet.''

"Kiss me.''

She eagerly obliged as he turned for the stairs that led up to his room.

The next day was Friday, the final day before the wedding.

Adora had closed her shop, and Jed planned to stay home as well. They'd have this last day to be with the family and tie up any loose ends of their wedding preparations. And then tomorrow, after the ceremony and reception, they'd head for Tahoe and a three-day honeymoon. Lottie and Bob had said they'd be glad to stay a little longer to look after Tiff.

They all had breakfast together at the Church Street

house: Adora, Jed, Tiff, Lottie and Bob. In the distance, more than once, they heard the rumbling roar of a Harley.

"My," murmured Lottie as she shook powdered sugar onto her French toast. "There certainly do seem to be a lot of loud motorcycles around this morning."

Adora didn't dare look at Jed for fear she'd burst into a ridiculous fit of giggles.

Deirdre, the third Beaudine sister after Cat and Adora, arrived with her husband, Eddie, and their three daughters, Penny, Shannon and Rose, at a little before ten. Phoebe, her husband, Paul, and their two boys showed up not long after that. Both families would be spending the night at the big house Dillon and Cat owned out on Barlin Creek Road. But for now, of course, the whole idea was to be where the action was. So the little house on Church Street was packed with people.

There were a few awkward moments right after Adora introduced Jed. Both Phoebe and Deirdre kept slipping him wary, sideways looks. But within a few minutes, when they saw that their mother seemed to be putting up with him, they both relaxed and decided to go ahead and have a good time.

Right before the others arrived, Lottie had begun whipping up batch upon batch of her world-famous brownies to take to the reception. Lottie had always insisted that eating her brownies brought luck. So she planned to have lots of luck to pass around with the wedding cake tomorrow.

As the first batch began to bake and the tempting aroma filled the kitchen, Phoebe and Deirdre launched into a loving reminiscence of those great cookies with the M&Ms in them that Adora used to make years ago.

"Would you make 'em, Dory?" Phoebe begged, sounding almost like a kid again. "Would you make 'em, if Dee and I go out and get all the stuff?"

Adora graciously agreed that she would. So her two younger sisters headed over to the Superserve Mart to buy ingredients, leaving their children at the house under the supervision of their husbands. However, Paul and Eddie were actually out in the garage with Jed getting a rundown on the modifications he'd made to his Harley. Naturally Phoebe's boys started picking on Deirdre's girls. So the men came inside to handle the problem and then settled down to watch "Golden Universe of Sports" with Bob.

Adora was passing around a plate of brownie samples when the doorbell rang. She glanced up, thinking it must be Cat and Dillon. Jed was already striding toward the door.

He pulled it open. Morton Laidlaw waited on the other side.

Nine

Adora hurried across the room to Jed's side.

"I, um, wonder if I could have a word with you in private?" Morton asked the question in his usual hesitant, browbeaten way. His glance flickered to Adora. "Er, perhaps you should hear this, too, my dear."

"A word about what?" Jed spoke quietly, as always. But no one would mistake the hostile set to his jaw.

From the kitchen Adora heard Tiff's laughter. The sight of Charity's husband would only worry the girl. She put her hand on Jed's arm.

He looked at her. "Yeah?"

Adora tipped her head, indicating the houseful of relatives behind them. "Let's just step out on the porch, why don't we?"

"Fine." They joined Morton on the porch, and Adora quietly pulled the door shut behind them. Then Jed instructed, "All right. Say what you have to say."

Morton nervously scratched his weak chin and smoothed his balding crown. "I, well, first, there's something I want you to know."

"What?"

"As far as what happened all those years ago, when you and Dawn were in high school, I—"

Jed swore.

"Please. Won't you hear me out?"

Adora squeezed Jed's arm. "Jed..."

Jed dragged in a breath. "All right. Fine. Say what you have to say."

Morton shuffled his feet, then forced himself to continue. "It's only that, well, I've always felt at least partially responsible for what happened back then." He licked his lips, as if they'd suddenly gone dry. "The truth is, I should have stepped in. I knew very well, as did everyone else in town, that Dawn cared deeply for you. But I was too intimidated by my own wife. I allowed her to frighten poor Dawn into accusing you of an act you had never committed. And then I allowed Charity to call the police and have you taken away."

Now Jed wore a baffled frown. "I don't get it. What is this?"

Morton coughed twice and stroked his chin again. His hand shook. "I'm trying to make you see that I know my own part in what Charity did. And Dawn, well, she has always felt terrible about what *she* did to you."

Jed scoffed at that. "Yeah. Right."

"It's true," Morton protested. "She's always wished she could make amends some way. And so she has stayed in town the past week, since your mother's funeral."

"To do what?"

"To help me convince Charity to drop this ridiculous

custody suit she's so intent on. We—that is, Dawn and I—just don't think it's right. If Tiffany wishes to stay with you, then Charity shouldn't be allowed to take her away. Of course, Charity is never easy to convince. But we've been relentless. And we've finally succeeded.''

Jed blinked. ''You've what?''

''We've persuaded Charity to drop the suit. You should be getting a call soon from Wanda Spooner. Wanda will tell you that there'll be no custody battle after all.''

Adora could hardly believe her ears. ''Is this really true?''

''Yes,'' said Morton. ''It is.''

Jed remained unconvinced. ''No one ever talks Charity Laidlaw into backing off.''

Morton looked grim. ''Don't imagine it was easy. In the end, I'm afraid, I was forced to threaten divorce if she kept on with this. And, of course, if I divorced her, she'd lose a good deal of her edge over you as a potential guardian.'' A ghost of a smile haunted his thin lips. ''Now, wouldn't she?''

Jed grunted. ''Come on. You'd never do that.''

''I will if I have to.''

Jed peered at him more closely. ''For some reason, I'm actually startin' to believe you.''

''Whether you believe me or not, it's the truth. Quite frankly, the last thing I need in my old age is an ugly court battle, culminating in assuming custody of a child who doesn't want to live in my house in the first place. I've worked hard for my retirement, thank you. And I plan to enjoy it. So yes, I most definitely would have divorced Charity, should she have insisted on going through with this thing.''

Adora spoke up again. "But she's *not* going through with it. Right?"

"Right. It's all settled now. Our lawyer has been notified. Dawn has returned to Santa Barbara. And Charity is very angry with me." Morton sighed then, and his narrow shoulders drooped a little. "But that's nothing new, now, is it? In fact, divorce may be the only solution for the two of us, anyway. In the end."

For a moment Morton's watery eyes looked far away and very sad. He sighed once more and shook his head. "I've said more than I should have." He glanced from Jed to Adora and back to Jed again. "And I realize it's a busy time for you. But I just thought you'd want to know right away. Moreover, I've always felt that I owed you an apology."

"Is this it?"

"Yes. It is."

Jed looked at the older man long and hard. "All right, then. Thanks." He offered his hand.

Morton took it. "Best of luck to you." He nodded at Adora. "And to you, too, my dear."

Jed and Adora remained on the porch as Morton went down the walk and out to the street, where he climbed into his car. As he drove off, two black-clad riders roared by on big, gleaming machines. At the sight of Jed, they raised their fists high in a salute. Jed shot a fist skyward in return.

Then he turned to Adora. "What do you think?"

"About Morton?"

He nodded.

"He seemed sincere."

"I want to trust him."

"But?"

"But I can't help wondering if it might be some kind of trick."

Adora suggested, "We could try calling Wanda. But there's no privacy at all in the house. Maybe from your room."

"Good idea." He grabbed her hand and pulled her down the steps, up the driveway and in through the open door to the garage. They hurried up the stairs to the room above.

He dialed Wanda's number as soon as the door was safely closed. Adora waited, every nerve humming, as Jed explained what Morton had told him. She wished fervently that she could hear Wanda's end of the conversation.

"All right, fine. Thanks," Jed said at last. He hung up.

Almost before the phone hit the cradle, Adora was demanding, "Well?"

"Wanda says she hasn't heard anything."

"So what happens next?"

"She promised to call Charity's lawyer and get right back to us."

"How long will that be?"

"Who knows? A half hour if we're lucky. Or if the lawyer's unavailable, maybe not till next week. All she said was that as soon as she learns anything, she'll call back."

Adora let out a little groan. "Great. We get to live in suspense."

Jed put an arm around her and dropped a light kiss on the top of her head. The contact felt good, so she leaned into him and gave him a smile.

"Look," he said. "Let's go back to the house. If we

sit around up here, someone's bound to come looking for us."

"You're right." She lifted her mouth, and he brushed a kiss across her lips. "Let's go."

They trooped back down the stairs and went in through the kitchen, where various children played on the floor and Lottie stood at the sink, elbow deep in soap suds.

Tiff was over near the stove, cutting a tray of brownies. She turned when she heard them come in. "What are you two doing?"

Adora put on a bright smile. "Nothing much."

"Well, come on then. We could use your help."

"Yes," Lottie chimed in as she washed out a mixing bowl. "Get to work."

Jed murmured, "See you later," and escaped to the living room to join the rest of the men.

Not long after that, Deirdre and Phoebe returned with all the necessary goodies for the cookies Adora had promised to make. Adora set right to work assembling the ingredients. But she was all thumbs. Right off she dropped a glass measuring cup and broke it.

Lottie shooed the children out of the way and bustled over with the broom and dustpan. "Be more careful, honey."

"Yes, Mom."

But Adora's ears felt like they were twitching, she was listening so hard for the phone to ring. And she had trouble keeping her mind on the task at hand. When she opened the big bag of M&Ms, they went flying all over the place. Phoebe's younger son, Bruce, and Deirdre's Shannon were crawling around the floor at the time. They crowed in delight and began chasing the rolling treats.

"Don't eat off the floor," Lottie instructed. The children ignored her. Lottie put her hands on her hips and frowned at Adora. "Are you all right?"

"I'm fine, Mom. Just a little...excited, I guess."

Out on the street, several motorcycles thundered by, the riders gunning their engines as they went.

Lottie threw up her hands. "Well. I'm a wreck, I can tell you. Those awful motorcycles are driving me wild."

Phoebe, at the table, made a sound of agreement just as her son crawled by, still chasing M&Ms. Phoebe reached out, caught the child around the waist and put him on her lap. Phoebe looked at Lottie. "The town is wall-to-wall bikers, I swear." Bruce squirmed to be let down. "Sit still."

"Down, down. Mommy, down."

With a groan of resignation, Phoebe let Bruce go.

Lottie whimpered. "Wall-to-wall bikers. What does that mean?"

Phoebe explained, "We saw bikes parked all up and down Bridge Street. And on Commercial Row, in front of the Superserve Mart, there were at least fifteen of them, all in a long, shiny line. Dee and I mentioned them to Lizzie when she rang us up."

Deirdre, across the table from Phoebe, chimed in, "And Lizzie said they're all in town because of the wedding."

Lottie dropped to a chair and murmured faintly, "Pardon me?"

Adora knew that the time for explaining had come. But where to begin? "Oh, Mom. It's nothing to get excited about. The bikers are only here to pay their respects to Jed on his wedding day."

Lottie let out a small moan. "My daughter is having some kind of *biker wedding,* is that it?"

Adora went to her and put her arms around her. "Mom. Really. It's all perfectly harmless."

"How do you know that?"

"Jed's explained it all to me."

"Oh, I'm sure he has."

"Listen. You just can't believe all the old stories about bikers. These guys are only here to have a little fun."

"I was afraid you'd say that."

"Mom. It's going to be okay."

Lottie heaved a heartfelt sigh. "I hope you're right. I truly do."

"I *am* right. They'll hang out. They'll spend some money and make the local merchants happy. And then, after the wedding, they'll give us an escort out of town."

"Excuse me?"

"They'll ride behind us, when we leave for Tahoe. Lots of them. In double rows. To show respect, like I said."

Lottie shook her head. "Is this really happening?"

"Come on, Mom."

"May I have two aspirin?"

Adora kissed her mother's cheek. "Sure." She found the aspirin and gave them to Lottie. Then she returned to baking her cookies. She'd just popped the second cookie sheet in the oven when the phone rang.

Phoebe, who'd gotten up from the table to pour herself some coffee, reached out to answer.

"Don't touch that!" Adora didn't realize she'd shouted the command until she noticed how everyone in the kitchen turned to stare at her. She finished sheepishly, "I'll get it."

The second ring had just shrilled out when she picked it up. "Hello?"

"Hello. Adora?"

"Yes?"

"This is Wanda Spooner."

"Um, yes."

Jed had appeared from the living room. He came to stand beside her.

Wanda said, "I wonder if I could speak with Jed?"

"Yes. Yes, of course." Adora handed him the phone.

"Hello," he said warily. For a moment he listened to whatever Wanda had to say. Then he murmured, "Yeah. Thanks. Thanks a lot." And he set the phone gently back in its cradle.

He looked at Adora. She rolled her eyes as a signal that he shouldn't say anything he didn't want the world to hear. Phoebe, Deirdre, Lottie and Tiff were staring at him. Even Shannon and Bruce, who'd been playing patty-cake under the table, had stopped clapping their hands. Jed kept his mouth shut.

The silence in the room stretched out until Lottie couldn't take it anymore. "What is going on?"

Jed looked frantically at Adora, willing her to help him out. But her mind had gone as blank as a clean white sheet. So Jed was forced to face Adora's mother and put on a reassuring smile. "It's nothin', Lottie. Nothing at all."

"Who was that?"

"What?"

"On the phone?"

"Oh. On the phone."

Lottie just looked at him, shaking her head.

He bumbled on. "That was…just a friend. A friend who wants to, uh, borrow a blanket."

"A what?"

He looked away, his expression pained.

"What are you telling me, Jed?" Lottie prodded.

"Er, maybe you noticed that there's lots of bikers in town?"

Lottie made a harrumphing sound. "As if I could help it."

"Well, uh, one of 'em's an old buddy of mine."

"So?"

"So, he'll be sleeping at one of the local campgrounds tonight. And he forgot to bring his sleeping bag. So he called. From the Spotted Owl. Askin' if I could help him out." Jed looked at Adora and she stared back. He really was a terrible liar. He coughed. "Adora, maybe you should come help me pick out that blanket."

Adora whipped off her oven mitts and shoved them at Lottie. "Keep an eye on my cookies, will you, Mom?"

"Well, of course, but—"

They were out of there before Lottie could come up with a reason to stop them.

In Jed's room, Adora closed the door firmly and leaned back against it. "Well?"

Jed sucked in a big breath. "It's official."

Adora's chest felt like someone had tied a band around it. "What's official?"

"Charity's dropped the custody suit."

Ten

Adora could hardly allow herself to believe. "No..."

Jed was smiling. "Yes."

Elation filled her, lifting her.

And then Jed was grabbing her, spinning her around, raining kisses on her face, her hair, her chin, her throat. "Yes," he murmured between the kisses. "Yes, yes, yes, yes..."

She wrapped her arms around his neck, hooked her legs around his waist and hung on, turning her face up to his, giggling in pure joy. He kept spinning around. The whole world went in crazy circles.

And then, all at once, he stopped. Dizzy and still giggling, she stared at him.

"Adora," he said. Tenderly, he caught her lower lip between his teeth. She felt his tongue against the sensitive flesh.

"Oh..." It came out on a sigh.

His smile had changed. Now it was that special, intimate smile she'd come to know so well. And she was shimmering all over, changing into that naughty creature who lived for making love to him.

She tried to stop it before it was too late, reminding him, "We can't. The family—"

"Kiss me." His mouth hovered just above hers. And her whole body was wrapped around him. So close. She felt how he wanted her.

"Jed, I'm serious."

"So am I."

"They'll all be wondering what we're up to." Her voice sounded husky, though she'd meant to be firm.

He chuckled and pressed his hips upward, into her softness. "Let 'em wonder."

She groaned at the feel of him. Still, she tried to keep her head. "It's just…"

"What?"

"…not polite.…"

He chuckled again. And then he brushed his mouth back and forth against hers, driving her crazy, making her burn.

"Someone…" For a moment the feel of his lips skimming hers drove all thought from her mind. But then she caught herself and managed to finish "…will come looking for us."

He carried her the few steps to the door, reached out and engaged the privacy lock.

"Oh, Jed…"

"It won't take long. Say yes."

"Yes." The word escaped her lips before she could stop it.

And then there was no more chance to hold back. He strode to the bed and laid her down. Swiftly, he began turning her this way and that, peeling off her clothes. Within moments her dress and her sandals, her panties and her bra all lay in a heap on the floor. And she was completely nude.

Straddling her, he gazed down at her, his silver eyes as soft as the underside of a cloud in a summer sky. "It's a great day."

She nodded, her body singing and her heart as light as a sunbeam. "A wonderful day."

"You're so beautiful." He reached down and cupped her breast. "You are the softest woman. Smooth and soft." He bent close and laid a kiss between her brows as his hand trailed down, to her ribs, onto her belly.

She moaned in delight and then reminded him with just a trace of shyness, "You've still got all your clothes on."

"I know." He kissed her nose.

"Well, are you going to take them off?"

"You want me to take them off?"

She nodded.

He reared up tall again and loomed above her. His gaze moved over her, possessive and hot. "What the lady wants, the lady gets."

His hands went to his silver-buckled belt. Slowly he unhooked it, drew it from its loops. And then he whipped it over his head. When he let it go, it slithered through the air and landed on the floor atop her own discarded clothes. He took his shirt, gathering it slowly, and pulled it from his jeans, sliding it up his belly, over his chest and off. Then he reached behind him and tugged at the strip of leather that held back his hair. When the tie came free, he threw it on the pile with everything else. He tossed his head. His hair fell, wild and black as night around his shoulders. He still held his shirt. But not for long. He wadded it into a ball and pitched it toward the pile.

Adora lay beneath him, watching, thinking how she loved looking at him. He was so big and strong and wild, his silver cross gleaming, his hair in black coils on his powerful shoulders, like midnight silk.

He touched the top button of his fly and his expression turned teasingly grave. "You know, I could use a little help here."

She widened her eyes. "Help? From me?"

He nodded, slowly. "Uh-huh."

Equally slowly she pushed herself to a sitting position. They looked at each other, a long, deep look.

And then she helped him.

One by one, she undid the buttons of his battered jeans. She smoothed them wide, and he was free.

She saw his tattoo. She saw everything.

She touched him. And then she kissed him, the most intimate kind of kiss.

He groaned her name. She kissed him again, taking him deep.

She felt his hand, at the back of her head, guiding her, holding her steady as she pleasured him. His body strained to be closer. She went on, loving him that way, clutching his hard thighs for support, never wanting to stop.

But then his fingers fisted in her hair. He pulled her head back. She cried out a little at losing the silky feel of him in her mouth.

His eyes were so hot. White-hot. They were burning her.

"I want you now. I can't wait." His voice was the low, guttural purr of some huge and powerful animal.

All she could do was nod.

And it all happened so fast. He pushed her down and came into her, in one fluid, lightning move. He still wore his jeans and his boots. And neither of them cared.

She was wet and open and he filled her completely. She sighed in wonder and dazed delight. Even the slight friction from the fabric of his jeans only added to the pleasure, made the point of joining more acutely felt.

He moved—long, deep, consuming strokes. And she received him, totally, fully, lifting her legs to wrap them around his muscled back.

It went on forever, the best, the strongest, the most complete kind of loving, the way it had always been with Jed. Adora reveled in it, picking up the rhythms he set and giving back her own, finally forgetting where her body ended and his began. They were one.

At the finish they cried out in unison. And together they fell off the edge of the world.

A while later she reminded him softly, "We should get back downstairs."

He made a low noise of agreement.

But neither of them moved. They lay side by side on their backs. Adora turned her head to look at him. He was staring at the ceiling. Slowly he turned his head and met her eyes.

"I want to take a quick shower." She started to sit, but before she could do more than shift her body slightly, his hand shot out and closed over her arm.

With a tiny gasp of surprise, she looked back at him. "What?"

His palm slid down her arm until he found her hand. Forcefully he twined his fingers with hers. "I messed up. I didn't use anything."

She frowned, not quite following.

"No protection," he said.

She understood then, and worried her lower lip between her teeth. "Oh. I didn't even think…"

"Me, neither." He squeezed her hand, then brought it to his lips and kissed the back of it. "So tell me. What do you think about babies?"

She swallowed. "Babies?"

"Adora. What we just did could make a baby."

Defensiveness moved within her. "Well, I know that."

"We've never even talked about that. About kids."

She thought of her mother and her sisters, down in the kitchen, wondering what in the world she and Jed were doing up here for such a long time. "Jed. My family…" She gestured toward the door with the hand he wasn't holding. "We really do have to get back."

He just looked at her, a long look. "Let me put it another way. I want babies. I want them with you. Do you want them with me?"

"Jed, now is not the time to talk about this."

Again he was silent. And when he did speak, she wasn't prepared for what he said. "Do you want to call it off?"

Her heart seemed to stop. "What?"

"Think. Charity's out of the picture. Tiff can stay with me now, whether you and me get married or not."

Now her heart was beating too fast.

He had no patience with her silence. "Am I getting through here?"

She forced herself to speak. "Of course. You're right. We could call off the wedding. I just didn't, um, think about that. Until right now."

"So? Is that what you want? To call it off?"

"I..." Her mind was a blank. She hedged. "Do you?"

He let go of her hand. "What the hell do you think?" His eyes had darkened, like clouds before a storm. He swore, low and crudely. "I just told you I want to have kids with you." He looked at the ceiling again, as he lifted his hips off the bed and swiftly, angrily buttoned his fly. Then his eyes were on her once more. "Does that sound like I want to call it off?"

"Jed..."

"Answer me." He levered up on an elbow to confront her. "Does it sound like I want to call it off?"

She recoiled a little at the harshness of his tone, but then she sucked in a breath and said quietly, "No. No, I guess not."

"You don't get it." He actually sneered at her. "You just refuse to get it."

"What? Tell me. Get what?"

He only glared.

"Why are you so angry with me?"

He stiffened. And then, as abruptly as his rage had come, it left him. He dropped back on the pillow once more, turning his head away from her, toward the window, just as several motorcycles thundered by outside.

"Jed?" She dared to touch his shoulder.

He didn't respond, only lay there, staring toward the window. The sound of the motorcycles faded away.

"Jed..."

Still no response. Not knowing what else to do, Adora slipped off the bed and began collecting her clothes from the floor.

As she was shaking out her dress, he turned his head her way again. Instinctively she clutched the dress against herself in a self-protective gesture. But then she saw his eyes. They really didn't look angry anymore. She relaxed a little.

He spoke hesitantly. "It would still be better for Tiff. If you and me were together."

Almost before he got the words out, she heard herself eagerly agreeing. "Yes. Of course. It would be better for Tiff, much better. If we were a family." She couldn't figure out what he was thinking. He looked so serious. So grim.

And she felt so confused. She needed time, to think this through.

Yet in spite of her doubts, she kept babbling on. "We *have* gotten Tiff's hopes up, haven't we? I mean, it might be very hard on her, after losing her mother and all, to have us suddenly call off our wedding. Don't you think?"

He swung his booted feet off the bed and reached for his shirt. "Yeah. I already said I think it would be hard on her. But I gotta be honest. It's not on a par with having to go live with Charity. If you want to back out, she'll survive."

Adora stood where she was, clutching her dress against herself, trying to decide which course to take.

Though the basic reason for the marriage was no more, she couldn't imagine calling it off. Sending all the guests home. Going back to the way things had always been. Just Adora and her shop and her cute little apartment. Girls' nights out with Lizzie. And long phone calls from her mother, listening to her never-ending advice on how to snare the perfect man.

Jed had his arms in the sleeves of his shirt, but instead of yanking it on over his head, he was watching her. "It's your call, Adora."

She had to say something. "Well, okay. I think...we should just go on." There. She'd made a decision.

He said nothing.

She hastened to add, "We should go ahead with it, for Tiff's sake. Just go ahead and go through with it. Okay?"

He watched her for a moment more, then muttered, "Fine." He put the shirt over his head, pulled it down and tucked it in. Then he grabbed his belt and began threading it through his belt loops.

Outside, more bikes rumbled by. Adora stood not three feet from Jed, yet he seemed a thousand miles away. She wanted to reach out, to touch him, to reassure herself that the distance she felt between them was only an illusion. But somehow she didn't dare. And there was no time right then, anyway.

She murmured, "We really have to get back."

His lip curled in irritation as his gaze flicked over her. "I'm not the one standin' here naked." He spoke with heavy sarcasm. And it hurt.

The hurt must have shown on her face, because his hard expression softened a little. He dragged in a breath and let it out slowly. "Sorry. I guess I'm not too thrilled about this situation. All those people down there. And we've gotta deal with 'em, when what we need is the time to work this thing out."

She tried a smile, though it felt a little wobbly. "We can talk more tonight after things settle down. I promise."

"All right."

Sheepishly she suggested, "I really would like a quick shower."

"No one's stopping you." He bent and picked something up off the floor: the leather strip that he used to tie back his hair.

She stepped forward, laid her hand on his arm. "Will you wait for me?"

He looked down at where she touched him, then up into her eyes. A spark of heat arced between them, the way it so often did when they touched. "I'll wait. But don't take forever."

"I won't." She released his arm and fled to the bathroom, where she washed without getting her hair or face wet. She was dressed and ready to go in less than five minutes.

When she returned to the bedroom, he was sprawled in the chair in the corner, his hair once more neatly tied back. She noticed that he'd straightened the bed.

"Ready?"

She nodded.

He stood and turned for the door.

Activity stopped when they entered the kitchen.

Lottie had just put a sheet of cookies into the oven. "Well." She closed the oven door and turned to face Adora and Jed. "That certainly took long enough." Lottie waited, clearly expecting some explanation from one or the other of them. When none was forthcoming, she prodded, "Did you take care of it, then?"

Jed frowned. "Take care of what?"

"That blanket? Did you get that blanket for your friend?"

"Oh." Jed lifted a shoulder in a shrug. "He changed his mind. He doesn't need it after all."

"But I don't—"

Phoebe, who was standing right next to the stove herself, elbowed Lottie in the ribs and muttered out of the side of her mouth, "Mo-ther..."

Another motorcycle roared by on the street.

Lottie put the back of her hand against her forehead. "Oh, all right. I can't keep up with what goes on around here, anyway. Lord knows why I even try."

Adora felt the brush of Tiff's hand on her shoulder. "Are you guys all right?"

She manufactured a smile. "We're fine."

"Yeah," Jed mumbled. "Just fine."

More motorcycle engines thrummed outside. And this time they got closer and closer, until it was obvious they weren't going to pass on by. Deirdre, at the sink, looked out the window. "Two of them," she said. "They're in the driveway." The bikes in question roared out in unison as their riders gunned the engines, and then silence fell.

Adora sent a questioning look Jed's way. He shook his head.

At the window Deirdre said, "They're taking off their helmets." And then she let out a shriek. "Oh, no! I don't believe it!"

"Oh, my heavens what?" Lottie cried.

"It's Cat! Cat and Dillon!"

Everybody filed outside to ooh and ahh over Cat and Dillon, each dressed in black leather, each astride a big, black touring bike trimmed in red.

Cat laughed and tossed her short white-blond hair as she swung off her bike. "Dillon said there would be bikers all over the place."

"Yeah," Dillon agreed. "I thought we'd ride, too. In honor of the occasion." With some difficulty, due to old injuries, he climbed off the bike, leaving his helmet, as Cat had, between the saddlebag compartments behind the seat.

Jed stepped right up and offered his hand. "Welcome."

Dillon murmured, "Congratulations, man."

"Thanks." The two men shook.

Cat held out her slim arms toward Adora. "Get over here."

Adora ran to her, sighing when her big sister's arms went around her. "I'm so glad you're here."

"Me, too." Cat pulled back.

For a moment the sisters looked at each other. Then Cat frowned. And Adora knew her older sister had picked up all the anxious feelings she was trying so hard to hide.

"Adora?" Cat said her name carefully. "What—?"

Adora didn't let her finish. "Oh! I've got cookies in the oven. Mom's been watching them, but it's really my job."

"But—"

Adora was already in the garage, almost to the kitchen. She kept on going, through the side door and straight to the stove. She was bent over the oven when the rest of the women trooped inside.

A glance out the window showed her that Dillon and Jed were going over the touring bikes inch by inch. Dillon seemed to be doing most of the talking. No doubt he was lovingly detailing whatever modifications he'd made. Adora knew what would happen once they were through with the touring bikes; they'd move on to Jed's Softail in the garage. And it would be Jed's turn to explain about all the changes he'd made to the forks and the transmission, the pipes and the frame. Adora smiled, looking at the two dark heads bent close together. For a moment she almost forgot her inner turmoil over the marriage that didn't need to take place anymore.

But then as she turned back to the stove, her gaze locked briefly with Cat's. And all her apprehensions came rushing back. She wanted to talk with Cat. She *longed* to talk with Cat. Cat always understood. And Cat never judged.

However, it seemed that Jed was the one she should be talking to. And they *would* talk about it. Tonight. After everyone else had gone off to bed. They would work it all out then. She just had to wait, that was all.

So she avoided Cat. She stayed clear of her older sister all through lunch and the brief trip over to the church, where they held a simple wedding practice, with Bob giving the bride away and Tiff, the only attendant, walking down the aisle ahead of Adora.

Through the lunch and the rehearsal, it seemed to Adora that Jed hardly looked her way. When she stood beside him at the altar where tomorrow they would say their vows, he didn't meet her eyes. And he didn't touch her, either.

Not that he had to. This was just a rehearsal. All they had to do was stand in the right place.

But it wasn't like him not to touch her. Ordinarily, he touched her whenever he got the chance. As she touched him. Touches that weren't really even about how much they wanted each other. Touches that were about...affection. About caring. He would lay his arm across her shoulders. Or she'd brush his hand in passing. She had never thought about how physically devoted they had become with each other. Until now. When suddenly they weren't.

When she turned from the altar, Adora caught Cat

watching her again. Cat wore that worried frown on her face.

Adora looked away from her sister. She put on a bright smile and told herself that everything was going to work out fine.

When they returned to the house after the rehearsal, the men decided to play cards. They pulled the card table from the hall closet and set it up in the middle of the living room. Jed brought out the cards and poker chips. And Adora and Lottie whipped up a few munchies for them to snack on.

Everybody seemed to be making themselves comfortable. Jed had even gone so far as to change from his big black boots to the moccasins he liked to wear sometimes around the house. Dillon followed suit, taking off his own boots and anteing up in his stocking feet.

Phoebe and Deirdre put the kids down for naps in Lola's room, and the women settled in the kitchen to laugh and talk and drink iced tea. Everyone seemed content.

And Adora had a splitting headache.

Lottie's hand covered hers. "Honey, go lie down."

"Oh, Mom..."

"Go on. You've worked like crazy for two weeks. You deserve a few minutes' rest."

Adora looked around the kitchen. Brownies and cookies covered every inch of counter space; the baking was done. The lunch dishes had been washed and put away before they left for the church. "I think maybe I just will."

"Yes, go on. Go ahead," her sisters urged.

So she trudged up to the bedroom over the garage. In the bathroom there, she found some aspirin and took two of them. Then she returned to Jed's room, kicked off her sandals and stretched out on the bed.

For a moment she found herself looking at Jed's boots, lined up by the chair in the corner, where he must have left them when he changed to his moccasins. And then she closed her eyes.

She'd just about drifted off when she heard a knock at the door. With a weary sigh, she swung her feet to the floor and sat on the edge of the bed. "Yes?"

The handle turned and the door swung inward.

It was Cat. "Hi."

The sisters regarded each other.

And Adora couldn't stop herself. She moaned. "Oh, Cat..."

Cat came in, shut the door behind her and approached the bed. She sat beside Adora and put her arm around her. Adora let out a long breath and slumped against her big sister.

Cat squeezed Adora's shoulder. "Okay. What's going on?"

"I really shouldn't..."

"Sure you should. I'm your sister. Tell me what's wrong."

Adora sat a little straighter and met Cat's eyes. "I'm just, well, I'm really confused."

"About what?"

Adora threw up both hands. "Everything."

"Explain."

Adora opened her mouth, then shut it. As much as she loved and trusted Cat, it was Jed she should be talking to. And she knew it.

"Adora?"

Sighing, Adora got up. She went around the end of the bed to the far side, where the window looked out over the driveway. She stared down at the twin touring bikes, at all the shiny black paint and polished chrome gleaming in the afternoon sun.

"Come on, Adora." Cat rose from the bed and went around to stand next to her. "Whatever it is, it can be worked out." She took Adora by the shoulders and guided her backward, sitting her on the bed again, but on the far side now, facing the window that looked out on the street.

Adora leaned against Cat's slim strength once more and rested her head on Cat's capable shoulder. "Oh, I don't know. I just don't know…"

"You don't know what?"

And all at once, it was just too much of an effort *not* to tell Cat everything. She really could trust Cat. With her life, with all of her secrets.

"I just don't know if I should marry Jed."

Cat pulled back enough to give her a long look. "Why don't you know?"

And from there, it all came spilling out. Adora told Cat about Charity and the custody suit and how the real reason she and Jed had decided to marry was so he could be sure Charity wouldn't get Tiff. "I really do like Jed. A lot. And I respect and admire him in so many ways. Everything was working out just fine…"

"So what's the matter?"

She explained about Morton Laidlaw showing up at the door. "He told us Charity won't be suing for custody, after all. We checked out his story, just in case it might have been some kind of trick. But it wasn't. It's true. The lawsuit is off. We don't *have* to get married."

"Wait a minute. So then, as of now, is the wedding on or off?"

"It's on. We decided to go ahead with it, anyway, that it would be the best thing for Tiff."

"For Tiff," Cat repeated softly.

"Oh, Cat..."

"I'm listening."

"It's just that everything seems so...strange, all of a sudden. Jed's a million miles away. And I'm confused. Oh, I don't know. I just don't know...."

"Dory, when you called to tell me you were marrying him, you said you loved him."

Adora smoothed her skirt over her knees. "I...we agreed we'd say that, to make the marriage look as real and solid as possible."

"So you mean you don't love him?"

Adora let out a groan.

Cat spoke firmly. "Just answer the question. Do you love him?"

Adora couldn't answer. Helplessly she looked at her sister.

And as she stared at Cat, her old dream rose up.

Adora closed her eyes, imagining that she saw him: Mr. Wonderful in his Brooks Brothers suit. She couldn't see his face, of course. He didn't have a face. Because she'd never found him. But one thing was certain. He would never have Jed's face.

Because Jed would never wear a suit. Jed would dress in denim and black leather and big, mean boots. He'd wear his hair too long and a diamond stud in his ear, and he would ride his Harley until the day they laid him in the ground.

"Dory, you're stalling."

"All right, all right." She opened her eyes and straightened her shoulders. "It's just that it's all happened...so fast. Lola dying. And Jed and me getting together. He's been like a...a runaway train, roaring through my life. He's—'' She felt her face flaming.

Cat stroked her hair, soothing her. "What? Go on. Say it. You know you can say anything to me."

"I know, but— Oh, Cat. I've been such a phony."

"No..."

"Yes. I have. Remember, when I was with Farley?"

Cat made a growling sound. "The rat."

Adora patted her hand. "You're so loyal."

"He was nothing. A zero."

"Right. But remember, how I— Well, I did think I would marry him. And I, um, went to bed with him."

Cat cast a glance at the ceiling. "I remember. You'd have thought you invented sex. Going on and on about how wonderful it was. Even buying me a box of you-know-whats, so I could be safe and smart if I ever decided to take the plunge myself."

Adora groaned in embarrassment. "I can't believe I did that."

"But you did."

"I know. And it was all a big act."

Cat sat back a little. "What did you say?"

"It was an act. I *hated* making love with Farley. It was just...yuck. Just total yuck. I said I liked it so much because I was trying to convince myself I did. But I didn't. Deep inside I was sure that I could never enjoy...that kind of thing."

"I see."

"But then, with Jed..." She was blushing again.

Cat understood. "Another story altogether, huh?"

Adora nodded slowly. "Words cannot describe."

Cat lifted a brow. "So this is a problem?"

"No. Of course not. It's great. Terrific. But..."

"But what?"

"Well, I can't help wondering. Is it just, you know, physical? Is that all it really is? I mean, the truth is, Jed is just nothing like the man I've been dreaming of all these years. There really is a lot of outlaw in him. I never know what he might do. He can be so rough. And blunt. And crude, even. And you know I always pictured myself with someone who wanted the finer things in life and intended to go out and get them. But I'd put that dream man out of my mind. I honestly had. Until..."

The deep, soft voice finished from behind them. "...this morning when Morton Laidlaw showed up at the door."

Cat gasped. Adora froze. And then she turned.

Jed was there in the doorway. Wearing those moccasins that hadn't made a sound on the stairs. She had no idea how he'd gotten the door open without her hearing. But he had. Dillon stood right behind him.

How much had they heard? Way too much, judging by the bleak look in Jed's eyes.

"We, uh, wondered where the hell you two got off to," Dillon said.

"And now we know," Jed added with horrible finality.

Adora stood. But before she could so much as whisper Jed's name, he put up a hand, demanding silence. Then he flicked a glance from Dillon to Cat.

Dillon took the hint. "Come on, Cat." With a sharp movement of his head, he indicated the stairs.

Cat hesitated.

"It's okay," Adora said in a tight whisper. "You go on."

Cat opened her mouth as if to speak, then seemed to think better of the idea. She rose and went around the end of the bed toward the door. Jed stepped out of her way. He closed the door behind her the moment she went through it.

Adora remained on the far side of the bed. She felt rooted to the spot.

Jed said, "You should have waited. Talked to *me*."

"I know." The two words came out low and ragged, more air than sound.

"I told you. That first night I brought you up here to this room. Never to betray me."

All she could do was nod.

"But you did. Just now. You talked to *her*. Your sister. You told her everything. All the things you didn't have the guts to say to me."

"Jed—"

He raised his hand again, swift and hard, commanding silence, causing her words to freeze in her throat.

He went on, "You said you couldn't talk to me. That your family was waiting. But then you came up here. And you spilled your guts to her."

"Jed, I—"

He stopped her this time with just a look. "It's the same, Adora. Can't you see? The same as what Dawn did to me."

"No..."

"Yeah. The same. Okay, you're not cryin' rape. But you won't stand up beside me. Not really. You're hot for me. You'll say you love me to get what you want from me. But it's only a game to you, because in your heart you put me beneath you."

"No, Jed. You have to listen—"

"No. You listen. Get this. You can't say you love me for real. Because you don't love me. I know it. But I do love you."

Her heart felt like a hard fist grabbed it and squeezed. "I...what?"

"I love you. You're a good woman. You were good to Ma and you're good to Tiff. But it's not only that. It's...it's you. You, in your little flowered skirts and your pink underwear. You, lookin' up at me with those green eyes that don't know how to lie. I don't know how you did it, but somehow, you got yourself into my heart. And I love you. But it's never gonna work. I can see that now."

"But I don't...I can't—"

"Look." He sounded resigned. "Would you do something for me? One last thing?"

She stared at him, her mind frozen, not working. "What?"

"Would you look out for Tiff? Just for a day or two. I gotta get away, get my head on straight, you know?"

"But Jed..."

He dropped to the chair in the corner, kicked off his moccasins and pulled on his boots.

Adora struggled to absorb what was happening. "Jed. What are you doing? We, um, we really have to talk."

He cast her one quick, flat glance. "The time for talkin's past."

"But Jed, I—"

He stood. "Just answer my question. Will you look after Tiff for a little while?"

"Of course I will, but—"

He didn't let her finish. He was already at the door. "Thanks." He pulled it open. And then he was gone. She heard the echo of his boots on the stairs.

A moment later she heard his bike roar out.

And that did it. She understood then.

She had lost him.

Betrayed him and lost him.

And in losing him she knew the truth.

"Jed," she murmured aloud to the empty room. "I, um, I do. I love you. Jed. I do…"

She saw herself for what she was then: a complete fool. Looking for love so desperately for all those years. And then, when love finally found her, throwing it away.

Down in the garage, Jed gunned the bike's engine. And that mobilized her. She tore across the room, out the open door and down the stairs.

He was rolling out onto the street when she got to the garage.

"Jed!" She ran after him.

But he didn't hear. Or he didn't want to hear. He roared off toward Bridge Street.

"Jed! Jed wait! Please wait!"

He didn't turn. The bike was so loud and picking up speed. She'd barely made it to the street when he rounded the corner, going the opposite direction from her shop, headed for the highway that led out of town.

But she ran after him, anyway, as fast as her feet would take her, down to the corner, onto Bridge Street, past rows of gleaming choppers and their owners, who were hanging out on the sidewalk. They all turned to watch, all the bikers and their mamas, as she chased the Midnight Rider in her bare feet through the center of town.

"Jed! Oh, please…"

There were catcalls and whistles. Adora ignored them. She ran on, pounding past River Street and Buckland Avenue, though the distance between her and the man on the motorcycle grew and grew. The moment came when she lost sight of him. He vanished around the curve of the highway that led out of town. It was like having her heart ripped from her body. Still, she kept running, hoping, trying...

At last, her lungs burning and her feet like twin slabs of lead, she stumbled to a stop on the side of the road, at the very edge of town. The blood thundered in her veins; she commanded it to be silent. Her lungs screamed for air; through sheer will, she held her breath.

She stood perfectly still, staring off the way he had gone, listening for the sound of his engine. She heard it, a distant rumbling.

Which faded to a far-away whisper.

And finally became nothing at all.

Eleven

———

Adora walked back down Bridge Street with her head held high. There were more whistles and rude remarks from the bikers. Adora hardly heard them. All she could think about was Jed.

At the house her mother, her sisters and Tiff were waiting outside.

Her mother rushed to meet her when she reached the front walk. "Adora? Honey, what's happened?" She looked down at Adora's bare, dirty feet. "Sweetheart, you ran out without your shoes..."

Adora had no idea what to say. So she didn't say anything.

Tiff stepped forward. "He's gone?"

Adora nodded.

"But where did he go?"

"I...don't know."

Tiff's eyes filled with frightened tears. "You don't know?"

Adora fought to collect herself. She understood what must be going through Tiff's mind, with her mother dead only two weeks and now Jed roaring off like that.

She put her hand on Tiff's arm. "He'll be back, Tiff."

Tiff swiped at her eyes. "When?"

"Soon. He just, um, needs a little time."

"Oh, Dory." Tiff shook her head. "Something happened, didn't it? Something really bad."

Cat spoke up then. "Why don't you two go on upstairs? You can talk there."

Lottie sniffed. "Now wait a moment. I'd like to know—"

Cat already had Lottie by the arm. "We'll be in the house if you need us, Adora. Won't we, Mom?" She gave Lottie's arm a tug.

"But—"

"Come on."

Reluctantly Lottie acquiesced. Cat led her up the steps and in through the front door, with Phoebe and Deirdre following along behind.

By the time Adora and Tiff reached the room over the stairs, Adora had come to grips with the fact that she would have to tell Tiff the truth, at least as much truth as was suitable for the ears of an eleven-year-old girl.

So Adora closed the door and sat with Tiff on the bed and told the whole story as quickly and simply as she could.

She explained how Charity had hired a lawyer to take Tiff away from Jed. She said that she and Jed had decided to marry so that Jed could be sure not to lose Tiff. And she told of Morton's visit and what it meant.

Then came the hard part. Adora did the best she could with it.

"So it turned out we didn't need to get married, after all. But we were going to go ahead with it, anyway. Jed wanted to talk more about it. But I was thinking of everyone downstairs and how they'd be wondering where we were. So I put him off. And that hurt his feelings. And then, later, when I was taking a nap up here, Cat came to talk to me. And I told her everything. And Jed walked in while we were talking. And that *really* hurt him."

Tiff was shaking her head. "I don't understand grown-ups."

Adora struggled to make it all clearer. "Well you see, honey, Jed loves me."

Tiff rolled her eyes. "Well, I know that."

Adora gaped. "You do?"

Tiff grabbed her hands. "And you love him."

"Well. Yes. I do."

"So then you have to go find him. You have to say you're sorry and work things out. You have to bring him home."

Adora stared at Jed's sister. And then she grabbed her close. "Oh, Tiff. You are so right."

Tiff held on tight. "It's good you've got me to turn to when things get tough."

"Yes, it certainly is." For a moment they just hugged each other. Then Adora pulled back enough to meet Tiff's eyes. "But where could he have gone? What do you think? Maybe his cabin, out by the machine shop?"

"Uh-uh. If he really wants to get away, he's got to know that's the first place we'll go looking."

"Then where?"

"There are a lot of his buddies in town. Probably one of them will know."

A half hour later, Adora found one of Jed's buddies in the dim, smoky interior of the Spotted Owl Tavern. The man was bending over the jukebox, punching out songs.

"Er, excuse me. Spike?"

Slowly the biker turned. He was big—not as big as Jed, but powerfully built nonetheless. And unlike Jed, his tattoos were no secret. They ran up his forearms and over the sides of his bulging biceps. They were of snakes and bleeding hearts and daggers. They were for "Mother" and "Lilah" and "Suzie-Q."

The jukebox began playing "Light My Fire."

The biker slowly smiled, wider and wider, until Adora could see the silver crowns on his back teeth. "Well. How you doin', sweet thing?"

It was what he had called her last winter, when she and Cat had had that run-in with him.

She inched her chin up. "My name is Adora."

"You'll always be 'sweet thing' to me."

She decided to let the issue of what he called her pass. "I'm looking for Jed."

The biker burst into a loud guffaw. Nearby, his friend, the one known as Dooley, laughed too. From the speakers mounted in the corners around the room, Jim Morrison begged his baby to light his fire.

"The way I heard it," Spike sneered, "Jed ain't lookin' for you. Not anymore, anyways."

Adora refused to be ruffled. "It's important that I find him. Do you know where he is?"

"Everyone saw you, chasin' him out of town. Seems

to me like if he'd wanted to talk to you, he woulda let you catch him.''

Adora didn't flinch. "Do you know where he is, or not?''

Spike looked her up and down. "You know, if the Midnight Rider's through with you, maybe I'll give you a go myself.''

That did it. Adora spun on her heel and headed for the door.

"Hey, sweet thing.''

She froze.

He spoke to her back. "I know how to find him.''

She turned. "Where is he?''

His gaze crawled over her some more. "I'll take you there.''

"No, thanks.''

The biker lounged against the jukebox. "You want to get to him, you'll have to ride with me.''

"Maybe someone else will tell me where he is.'' She looked around the place. There were bikers at the pool table, and several more lined up at the bar, both men and women, all dressed in the biker style, denim and leather and heavy boots. As Adora scanned the room, each of those bikers looked at her levelly. And not one of them said a word.

Spike went right on smiling. "Like I said, you'll have to ride with me.''

Adora kept her shoulders back and her spine straight, even though a shiver traveled up the backs of her legs. She told herself firmly that she had nothing to fear from Spike. No biker would mess with the Midnight Rider's woman, she was sure of that. All she had to do was reach Jed. And everything would be fine.

"Make your choice, sweet thing.''

"All right. Let's go."

Spike grunted. "That little pink dress ain't gonna make it. You go change into somethin' you can ride in. Then you come on back here and me and Dooley'll take you to your man...if he still is your man."

"He is."

"Well, we'll see about that now, won't we?"

Adora rushed over to her apartment to change to old jeans, tennies and a T-shirt. From there, she called the house on Church Street. Tiff answered.

"Did you find out where he is, Dory?"

"I'm working on it. I promise. I'll bring him home safe. Now, is Cat there?"

Cat came on the line. "Hi."

"Hi. Listen. Remember Spike?"

"Who could forget him?"

"He says he knows where Jed is. And he's going to take me there."

"Oh, no."

"Cat, I have to do it. I'll be all right."

"Let me get Dillon. We'll come, too."

"No. I'm going to do this myself. It's important. It'll mean a lot to Jed. That I dared to come alone. I just...I feel that it will."

"It's insane."

"Cat, I'll be all right. All bikers respect Jed. Spike wouldn't dare do anything to me. But I just wanted you to know what I'm up to. Because I'll be gone for a little while."

"Don't do it, Dory."

"Cat. You're the best big sister in the world."

"God. Be careful."

"I will. Don't worry."

"Oh, yeah, sure."

"Wish me luck. And don't let anyone in the family leave town. I'll be back in time for my wedding."

"Right."

"And I'll be bringing the groom."

"Dory, you're crazy."

"I love you, Cat." Quietly she hung up. Then, grabbing an old jacket from a peg by the door, Adora headed for her rendezvous with Spike.

Twelve

She found Spike lounging on the seat of his chopper outside the Spotted Owl. Dooley waited nearby, along with most of the bikers who had been in the bar a half hour before.

"Borrowed you a helmet," Spike announced when she reached his side. He held up a hand toward the crowd. "Hey, Sadie, let's have it."

A woman in skintight leather pants and a matching bustier tossed a red helmet his way. He caught it neatly as it sailed for his head, then threw it to Adora. She put up her hands just before it hit her in the face. A few low chuckles issued from the crowd.

"Strap it on," Spike instructed.

Adora put on the helmet as Spike straddled his bike and put his own helmet on. Dooley did likewise. Then the men started up their bikes. The powerful engines roared out.

"Climb on!" Spike shouted over the roar.

Gingerly Adora mounted behind him.

"Wrap your arms around me!"

Reluctantly she slid her arms around his waist. He gunned the engine and then popped the clutch. The bike shot forward. Adora let out a shriek and held on for dear life. Spike guffawed.

After that he slowed it down until they got out of town. They rolled to the corner at a stately pace and turned onto Bridge Street, which seemed to go on forever, lined with what appeared to be hundreds of bikers and their gleaming machines. The bikers shouted and stomped.

Blessedly, Adora couldn't hear what they shouted. The two bikes drowned them out. She tried not to look at them. She stared straight ahead. She thought of Jed. She told herself that she would see him soon and that then everything would be all right.

But she didn't see him soon.

The trip took hours. And it was a hard, fast, bone-jarring ride. They headed West, through Portola and Blairsden and over to Yuba City, then south to the Central Valley by way of Lincoln and Roseville.

Every once in a while they'd roll into the parking lot of a rundown bar or road house. They'd cruise the lot, then roll back out, headed for the highway again. Though Spike didn't bother to explain what he was up to, Adora figured it out. He and Dooley were stopping at the places Jed might be, checking for his Softail parked among the other bikes.

But Jed's bike was never there. So the ride went on. Adora's ears rang and her bottom ached. And though the day was fading, it seemed to get hotter as they rode.

Adora wished she could take off her jacket, but she didn't dare let go of Spike. And, anyway, where would she put it if she did take it off?

They rode on, through Sacramento, and then down Highway 99, stopping only one time, near Turlock, for gas.

It was hot in Turlock, and the air felt parched dry, though it was twilight by then.

"I have to use the bathroom," she told Spike.

"Make it quick."

Adora dragged herself from the bike and waddled to the rest room as fast as her wobbly legs would take her. Once safely on the other side of the closed door, she swiftly took care of business.

When she went to the sink to wash her hands, she saw herself in the mirror. A small cry of dismay escaped her. She looked terrible. Her sweaty hair was plastered to her head from the helmet. Her mascara had slid down to make hideous smudges under her eyes. And beyond the way she looked, her hands and the lower part of her face, which where exposed to the wind, felt numb. Her bottom just plain hurt, and she wondered if the ringing would ever fade from her ears. Maybe she *was* crazy to have done this, just as Cat had said.

She heard a short, impatient rap on the door just as she was slurping water straight from the faucet. "Come on, sweet thing. Let's move."

With a sigh she wiped the smudges from beneath her eyes, washed her numb hands, put on her helmet and went out to climb up behind Spike once again.

They rode on, Spike and Adora in the lead, Dooley close behind. Night came but brought no relief from the August hcat in the semiarid heart of California. They went through Fresno. Some miles after that Spike took a side road. And then another side road and another.

The roads got dustier and the hour got later. Still they drove on, through tiny towns too small for Adora to figure out their names before they disappeared in a cloud of road dust beneath their wheels.

And then, a few miles out of one of those little towns, a light shone through the trees up ahead. They rounded a bend and came up on a low, rambling wood-sided shack painted an ugly, peeling green with a wide, sagging porch across the front. The faded neon sign on the roof read: Mama Maria's—Bar Eats Pool.

A long row of choppers waited in front of the porch. As Spike pulled in at the end of the row and Dooley rolled into the next space over, Adora eagerly scanned the bikes, looking for Jed's Softail.

Her heart jumped into her throat when she saw it.

At last. They had found him. Joy and relief washed through her. It would be all right now. It had to be.

Though her legs felt as numb as her bottom by then, Adora managed to get off the bike. She yanked off the helmet and then didn't know where to put it. Spike took it from her and set it on his bike with his own.

"Ready, Dooley?" Spike asked his buddy.

"You bet."

Spike tossed a tattooed arm across Adora's shoulders. "You come on inside, sweet thing. We'll see if the Midnight Rider's gonna claim you for his old lady. If he doesn't, well, then you always got me...."

Adora jerked back.

But Spike just laughed and held on.

Adora glared at him, trying to look tough, doing her very best not to think about all the things that might happen out here. In the middle of the night, several miles from Lord-knew-where, with the only familiar faces those of the leering Spike and his best buddy, Dooley.

She put on her most no-nonsense tone. "Let go of me, Spike."

But he only laughed again and yanked her closer, his arm turning to a vise around her neck. "Go easy, baby," he breathed into her ear. "It ain't gonna be long now."

Adora bit her lip and told herself she would not break down and cry.

Hauling her right along with him, Spike started for the side steps up to the wide veranda. She heard Dooley's boots following behind them.

As they moved toward the entrance to Mama Maria's, Adora kept up her struggle to pull free. But Spike held her in a grip of steel, close to his side. Every time she jerked away, he chortled in demented glee and yanked her up against him, tighter than before.

They stumbled at last to the door, where Spike lifted a boot and kicked the thing open. Then he dragged Adora inside.

The door swung shut behind them. Adora cast a desperate glance around, looking for Jed. She didn't see him, but she did get a good look at where Spike had brought her. It made the Spotted Owl look like a fern bar.

Except for the bare bulbs directly over the two pool tables, beer signs provided the main source of light. The air reeked of smoke, soured liquor and sweat. ZZ Top blared from the jukebox.

"Hey Spike, what you got there?" someone called from out of the gloom. "You gonna share?"

Frantically seeking silver eyes and midnight hair,

Adora searched the roomful of strange, hostile faces. Her terror was mounting, though she swore to herself she wouldn't show it.

Spike laughed some more and then answered the question about whether he would share. "I ain't decided yet." As he spoke his grip loosened a little.

Adora took the opportunity to shove him away.

He stumbled back, then caught himself. "Aw, sweet thing..." He stuck out his lower lip, pretending to be hurt. "That wasn't nice." His mean eyes narrowed. "You get back here."

"Leave her alone, Spike."

It was Jed's voice, low and gentle as always.

Adora whirled and saw him, in the shadows at the far end of the bar.

Spike met Jed's eyes. "I brought you your woman. *If* you still want her." Spike's lip curled in an ugly smile. "Well. Waddaya say? Is this woman yours or not?"

Adora held her breath.

And then Jed answered. "She's mine."

The air rushed back into her lungs.

Spike laughed long and hard. Then he grunted. "Just checkin'." He turned to Adora. "You gonna say thanks for the ride?"

She drew up her shoulders and held her head high. "Sure. Thanks. For the ride."

"You're welcome. Anytime." He turned to his friend. "Let's get drunk, Dooley." And the two of them headed for the bar.

Jed threw some money down and then elbowed his way to her side.

She watched him coming, thinking that he looked tired and just about as sweaty and dusty as she was. But still, the sight of him eased her, like a long drink of water would soothe a woman dying of thirst.

He stood before her. "Oh, Jed..." She reached for him.

He stepped back before she made contact. "Where's Tiff?"

"At home. Safe, I promise you."

He looked at her for a long moment, as if deciding whether to believe her or not. Then he shrugged. "Come on." His voice had no emotion in it. "You look beat. I'll take you somewhere to get some sleep. And tomorrow I'll see that you get home." He turned for the door.

Adora just stood there, staring after him, realizing with a sinking heart that nothing had changed. He shoved on the door and went through it. With a small cry she ran to catch up.

Outside, a full moon hung low over distant hills. The stars shone down. The heat had faded a little, now it was so late. Adora stood on the sagging porch of the road house, watching Jed back his bike out of the row.

When he was clear of the other choppers, he cast her an impatient glance. "You must have had a helmet, or some highway mounty woulda stopped you."

She moved to the set of steps that went down from the center of the porch, opposite the door. There was a peeling wood pillar there. She leaned against it and stared at Jed.

"Adora. Where's your helmet?"

She sighed. "Over there. On Spike's bike."

"Get it."

"Jed, listen, I—"

"Just get the damn helmet, and let's get out of here."

Feeling beaten, she turned and trudged the length of

the porch. He started up his bike, the sound like thunder in the peaceful night. She went down the side steps and got the red helmet.

"Move it!" he shouted, over the bike's rumbling roar.

She approached him.

"Climb on!"

And then she stopped.

"Come on, Adora!"

She couldn't help it. She had to know if there was any hope. She'd ridden for hours and hours. And she had a right to know. "Did you mean it, Jed? Am I still yours?"

He looked at her, then looked away. "Just get on."

She threw the helmet down in the dirt and shouted, "Jed, I was wrong to think for a second that my silly old dreams could hold a candle to what we have!"

"Adora—"

"No! Listen. Please, listen." She spoke loud and strong, strong enough that she knew he could hear every word, in spite of the bike's deafening roar. "The minute you turned and walked away from me, I admitted it to myself. I do love you."

Jed cast a glance toward the road house. Adora followed his gaze. They had company. The bikers from inside had filed out onto the porch to watch. She was long past caring that they'd drawn a crowd. She said it again. "Jed. I love you. I love you for real."

"Look, just get on the bike."

"No. I mean it. I love you. Please. Talk to me."

"Not here."

"Then where?"

"Yeah," one of the biker's called out. "If not here, then where, man?"

There was a murmur of agreement from the crowd.

"Adora…" Jed shook his head.

"Tell him again how you love him!" a rumbling voice instructed.

"Tell him you can't get enough of him!"

"Tell him you wanna ride with him till you can't ride no more!"

Adora sucked in a fortifying breath and faced all those dangerous characters. "Excuse me. This is private. Do you mind?"

But not one of the bikers moved.

She waved a disgusted hand at them and turned back to Jed. "All right. I'll tell you a thousand times. I love you. I…can't get enough of you. I…I want to ride with you…um…"

"Till you can't ride no more!" a helpful voice finished for her.

"Right," Adora agreed. "Exactly. Thanks."

"No problem," replied the voice.

Jed turned off the bike. He leaned on the handlebars.

Adora looked right at him and spoke straight from her heart. "I love you so much. I never knew I could love anyone like I love you. Maybe I was sort of a shallow woman, until you. A shallow woman knocking herself out trying to catch a shallow guy. But then there was you. And, oh, Jed. I knew it right away, that day on the Trout Creek Trail just before we found Lola. But I was so scared. To admit it to myself. And then Tiff fixed that. Because she needed me to marry you. It seemed so noble, to marry you for Tiff's sake. But now

I don't have to marry you for Tiff's sake. If I marry you, it'll just be because that's what I want to do. Because I love you. And like I said, it scares me how much I love you. But to lose you, that scares me more...."

He was listening. He was softening. She knew. She could tell.

She fell to her knees in the dirt. "Oh, Jed, please." Proudly she begged him. "What do you want me to do? I'll do anything. I swear to you."

"Anything?" Now a slight smile teased at the corners of his mouth.

Adora knew she was in for it. But she vowed, anyway. "Yes. I'll do anything you say. If you'll just be my husband. If you'll just stand beside me for the rest of our lives."

Now he really was smiling. And a wicked gleam had sparked in his pale eyes. He swung his leg off the bike and slowly sauntered over to her. He put down his hand.

She took it.

And then he hauled her close and kissed her as even he had never kissed her before.

On the porch the bikers burst into wild catcalls and raucous applause.

"All right, dammit," Jed whispered in her ear. "Maybe it will work, after all. You got class, heart and guts, Adora Beaudine. And I'm gonna love you like no woman's ever been loved. For the rest of our lives."

Two days later, after the ceremony and the reception, after Adora and Jed rode out of Red Dog City with a phalanx of bikers following behind them, after their wedding night in a fancy hotel in Tahoe, Jed took Adora to a certain tattoo parlor he knew of. There she kept her promise to do anything he asked.

It was only a small tattoo. In a place where no one but Jed would ever see it.

Of a heart.

And his name.

* * * * *

SILHOUETTE WOMEN KNOW ROMANCE WHEN THEY SEE IT.

And they'll see it on **ROMANCE CLASSICS**, the new 24-hour TV channel devoted to romantic movies and original programs like the special **Romantically Speaking—Harlequin™ Goes Prime Time.**

Romantically Speaking—Harlequin™ Goes Prime Time introduces you to many of your favorite romance authors in a program developed exclusively for Harlequin® and Silhouette® readers.

Watch for **Romantically Speaking—Harlequin™ Goes Prime Time** beginning in the summer of 1997.

If you're not receiving ROMANCE CLASSICS, call your local cable operator or satellite provider and ask for it today!

ROMANCE CLASSICS

Escape to the network of your dreams.

See Ingrid Bergman and Gregory Peck in *Spellbound* on Romance Classics.

Take 4 bestselling love stories FREE
Plus get a FREE surprise gift!

Special Limited-time Offer

Mail to Silhouette Reader Service™

P.O. Box 609
Fort Erie, Ontario
L2A 5X3

YES! Please send me 4 free Silhouette Desire® novels and my free surprise gift. Then send me 6 brand-new novels every month, which I will receive months before they appear in bookstores. Bill me at the low price of $3.24 each plus 25¢ delivery and GST*. That's the complete price and a savings of over 10% off the cover prices—quite a bargain! I understand that accepting the books and gift places me under no obligation ever to buy any books. I can always return a shipment and cancel at any time. Even if I never buy another book from Silhouette, the 4 free books and the surprise gift are mine to keep forever.

326 BPA A3UY

Name   (PLEASE PRINT)

Address   Apt. No.

City   Province   Postal Code

This offer is limited to one order per household and not valid to present Silhouette Desire® subscribers. *Terms and prices are subject to change without notice. Canadian residents will be charged applicable provincial taxes and GST.

CDES-696   ©1990 Harlequin Enterprises Limited

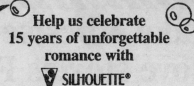

**Help us celebrate
15 years of unforgettable
romance with**

SILHOUETTE®

Desire

You could win a genuine lead crystal vase, or
one of 4 sets of 4 crystal champagne flutes!
Every prize is made of hand-blown, hand-cut
crystal, with each process handled by master
craftsmen. We're making these fantastic gifts
available to be won by you, just for helping us
celebrate 15 years of the best romance reading
around!

DESIRE CRYSTAL SWEEPSTAKES
OFFICIAL ENTRY FORM

To enter, complete an Official Entry Form or 3" x 5"
card by hand printing the words "Desire Crystal
Sweepstakes," your name and address thereon and
mailing it to: in the U.S., Desire Crystal Sweepstakes,
P.O. Box 9076, Buffalo, NY 14269-9076; in Canada,
Desire Crystal Sweepstakes, P.O. Box 637, Fort Erie,
Ontario L2A 5X3. Limit: one entry per envelope, one
prize to an individual, family or organization. Entries
must be sent via first-class mail and be received no later
than 12/31/97. No responsibility is assumed for lost,
late, misdirected or nondelivered mail.

DESIRE CRYSTAL SWEEPSTAKES
OFFICIAL ENTRY FORM

Name: _____

Address: _____

City: _____

State/Prov.: _____ Zip/Postal Code: _____

KFO

15YRENTRY

Desire Crystal Sweepstakes
Official Rules—No Purchase Necessary

To enter, complete an Official Entry Form or 3" x 5" card by hand printing the words "Desire Crystal Sweepstakes," your name and address thereon and mailing it to: in the U.S., Desire Crystal Sweepstakes, P.O. Box 9076, Buffalo, NY 14269-9076; in Canada, Desire Crystal Sweepstakes, P.O. Box 637, Fort Erie, Ontario L2A 5X3. Limit: one entry per envelope, one prize to an individual, family or organization. Entries must be sent via first-class mail and be received no later than 12/31/97. No responsibility is assumed for lost, late, misdirected or nondelivered mail.

Winners will be selected in random drawings (to be conducted no later than 1/31/98) from among all eligible entries received by D. L. Blair, Inc., an independent judging organization whose decisions are final. The prizes and their approximate values are: Grand Prize—a Mikasa Crystal Vase ($140 U.S.); 4 Second Prizes—a set of 4 Mikasa Crystal Champagne Flutes ($50 U.S. each set).

Sweepstakes offer is open only to residents of the U.S. (except Puerto Rico) and Canada who are 18 years of age or older, except employees and immediate family members of Harlequin Enterprises, Ltd., their affiliates, subsidiaries and all other agencies, entities and persons connected with the use, marketing or conduct of this sweepstakes. All applicable laws and regulations apply. Offer void wherever prohibited by law. Taxes and/or duties on prizes are the sole responsibility of the winners. Any litigation within the province of Quebec respecting the conduct and awarding of a prize in this sweepstakes may be submitted to the Régie des alcools, des courses et des jeux. All prizes will be awarded; winners will be notified by mail. No substitution for prizes is permitted. Odds of winning are dependent upon the number of eligible entries received.

Any prize or prize notification returned as undeliverable may result in the awarding of that prize to an alternative winner. By acceptance of their prize, winners consent to use of their names, photographs or likenesses for purposes of advertising, trade and promotion on behalf of Harlequin Enterprises, Ltd., without further compensation unless prohibited by law. In order to win a prize, residents of Canada will be required to correctly answer a time-limited, arithmetical skill-testing question administered by mail.

For a list of winners (available after January 31, 1998), send a separate stamped, self-addressed envelope to: Desire Crystal Sweepstakes 5309 Winners, P.O. Box 4200, Blair, NE 68009-4200, U.S.A.

Sweepstakes sponsored by Harlequin Enterprises Ltd., P.O. Box 9042, Buffalo, NY 14269-9042.

As seen on TV!
Free Gift Offer

With a Free Gift proof-of-purchase from any Silhouette® book,
you can receive a beautiful cubic zirconia pendant.

This gorgeous marquise-shaped stone is a genuine cubic
zirconia—accented by an 18" gold tone necklace.
(Approximate retail value $19.95)

Send for yours today...
compliments of ▼ *Silhouette*®
TM

To receive your free gift, a cubic zirconia pendant, send us one original proof-of-
purchase, photocopies not accepted, from the back of any Silhouette Romance™,
Silhouette Desire®, Silhouette Special Edition®, Silhouette Intimate Moments®
or Silhouette Yours Truly™ title available at your favorite retail outlet, together with
the Free Gift Certificate, plus a check or money order for $1.65 U.S./$2.15 CAN. (do
not send cash) to cover postage and handling, payable to Silhouette Free Gift Offer.
We will send you the specified gift. Allow 6 to 8 weeks for delivery. Offer good until
December 31, 1997, or while quantities last. Offer valid in the U.S. and Canada only.

Free Gift Certificate

Name: _____

Address: _____

City: _____ State/Province: _____ Zip/Postal Code: _____

Mail this certificate, one proof-of-purchase and a check or money order for postage
and handling to: SILHOUETTE FREE GIFT OFFER 1997. In the U.S.: 3010 Walden
Avenue, P.O. Box 9077, Buffalo NY 14269-9077. In Canada: P.O. Box 613, Fort Erie,
Ontario L2Z 5X3.

FREE GIFT OFFER   084-KFD
ONE PROOF-OF-PURCHASE
To collect your fabulous FREE GIFT, a cubic zirconia pendant, you must include this
original proof-of-purchase for each gift with the properly completed Free Gift Certificate.

084-KFDR